''Why don't you : [...]
saloon with me?'' L[...]
be right pleased to buy you a drink.''

''I wouldn't drink with the likes of you,'' snarled
Davey.

Faye spoke up again, saying, ''Please, Davey,
don't do this again—''

''Shut up!'' The young cowboy's hand flashed toward her face as she shrank back in her chair. Another instant and his palm would have cracked across
her cheek in a vicious slap.

His hand never got there. Fingers like iron clamped
painfully around his wrist, jerking it to a halt, and he
looked up with a surprised sneer into the face of the
stranger who had moved like lightning.

Longarm said quietly, ''You don't know how
much I wish you hadn't tried to do that, old son.''

TABOR EVANS

LONGARM

AND THE
ANGEL OF INFERNO

JOVE BOOKS, NEW YORK

LONGARM AND THE ANGEL OF INFERNO

A Jove Book / published by arrangement with
the author

PRINTING HISTORY
Jove edition / April 1996

The Putnam Berkley World Wide Web site address is
http://www.berkley.com

ISBN: 0-515-11843-5

A JOVE BOOK®
Jove Books are published by The Berkley Publishing Group,
200 Madison Avenue, New York, New York 10016.
JOVE and the ''J'' design are trademarks
belonging to Jove Publications, Inc.

PRINTED IN THE UNITED STATES OF AMERICA

10 9 8 7 6 5 4 3 2 1

Chapter 1

It was a little before eight-thirty in the morning when Longarm rode into the town of Inferno, Arizona Territory, not far north of the Mexican border. Despite the early hour, the sun was a bright ball of fire in a brassy sky and the temperature was already hotter than the hinges of Hades. This place was aptly named, Longarm thought as he looked around the small town.

Inferno's main reason for existing stood on stilt-like legs at the east end of the settlement. The big water tank was next to the tiny station building. The railroad had had to drill deep here to strike water, but they had found the precious stuff. When the trains came through every couple of days, they always stopped to fill the locomotive boilers. The tracks ran almost exactly due east and west, and the buildings of the town were constructed along the south side of the right-of-way, facing the tracks across a narrow street. The station itself was right beside the steel rails.

In addition to being a water stop on the Southern Pacific, Inferno also served as a supply point for the ranches in the distant hills to the north and the mines across the border in Sonora. Longarm counted three saloons, a couple of hash houses, a good-sized emporium, a hotel, a blacksmith shop, and a squarish, impressive building made out of stone blocks that had probably been quarried in Mexico and then

1

freighted up here—rather than the usual adobe or clapboard. He reined the tired dun to a halt in front of the building and read the sign over the door at the top of a short flight of steps: INFERNO—TOWN HALL—SHERIFF'S OFFICE—JAIL.

So that was the center of the local government, thought Longarm. He knew he ought to stop and let the local star-packer know he was in the vicinity, but at the moment he was just too damn worn out, not to mention hungry. He wanted a surrounding of grub in one of those cafes and then a soft bed in a hotel room for about ten hours. After that he might feel human enough to talk to the local law.

Longarm heeled the dun into a walk again. There were a few people on the street, a couple of wagons parked in front of the emporium. He felt eyes on him, and looked over to see two men on the porch of one of the saloons, watching him as he rode past. He gave them a nod, not too friendly, not too brusque. They probably took him for a drifting hard-case.

Not that he could blame them for reaching that conclusion. He wasn't all duded up the way he was back in Denver. He wore denim jeans that were gray with trail dust and a sweat-stained hickory work shirt with the sleeves rolled up a couple of turns on his brawny forearms. His snuff-brown, flat-crowned Stetson also showed signs of the long, hard pursuit that had taken him clear to the Mexican border from Colorado before it had ended futilely. He rode a Mc-Clellan saddle, so it was plain to see he wasn't a cowboy, and most miners didn't wear one of old Sam Colt's equalizers in a cross-draw rig hung for a speedy draw. That left either lawman or owlhoot, and with his grim expression and a week's worth of dark stubble on his jaw, Longarm didn't look much like a lawman.

He reined the dun to a stop again and swung down from the saddle in front of the establishment that somebody had imaginatively named the Inferno Cafe. The dun was played out too, and Longarm felt bad about not tending to him first. But his rations had run out about the middle of the previous day, and the horse had at least gotten to graze a little when

2

Longarm stopped to rest an hour or so before dawn. He'd been lucky enough to find a trickle of water in a gully with some tough grass growing alongside it. As soon as he got a meal here in the cafe, he would take the dun over to the livery barn he had spotted behind the hotel.

After looping the horse's reins around the hitch rack, Longarm stepped up onto the porch and opened the screen door. The smell of coffee and frying steaks and potatoes made his stomach clench in anticipation.

There were half a dozen tables in the place, and only one of them was occupied, although most of the stools at the counter were full. Longarm sat down at one of the empty tables, figuring he'd need some room to spread out all the food he intended to order. He took his hat off and dropped it on the chair next to him.

A waitress came out from behind the counter a moment later and approached the table. "Mornin'," she said to Longarm in a soft drawl that bespoke Southern origins. "What can I get you, mister?"

Longarm looked up at her and managed a smile despite his hunger and weariness. She was worth smiling at. She was a little bitty thing, not more than five feet tall, but the curves of her breasts and hips under the gray dress she wore were ample evidence that she was a full-grown woman. Thick chestnut hair fell to her shoulders, framing clean, wholesomely pretty features. Her eyes were a deep green, and they reminded Longarm of an oasis in the desert . . . an apt analogy considering the mostly barren landscape around Inferno.

"I'm tempted to say bring me two of everything you've got in the kitchen," replied Longarm, his smile widening into a grin. "I reckon if I did, though, I'd be proving that old saying about how a fella's eyes can be bigger than his stomach." He glanced at the menu chalked onto a board behind the counter. "Let's start off with a couple of steaks and some potatoes and a stack of flapjacks and maybe some biscuits and gravy. And coffee."

"Wouldn't it have been easier to just tell me what you *didn't* want?"

3

Longarm chuckled. "Maybe so. But I've been without grub since the middle of the day yesterday, and that ol' furnace of mine takes plenty of stoking."

The young woman let her eyes roam rather boldly over Longarm's rangy, powerful frame, then nodded. "I imagine it does," she said with a smile of her own. "I'll get the cook started on your order."

Longarm watched in appreciation the slight sway of her hips as she walked away. It wasn't a calculated motion, he sensed, just something natural about her, a part of her femaleness.

He took a deep breath and rolled his shoulders to get some of the stiffness out of them. Flirting with the pretty waitress had made him feel a little better already. Once he had eaten and gotten some sleep, the world would look a lot better.

Of course, he'd still have to go back to Denver and tell his boss, Chief Marshal Billy Vail, that the man he had been chasing for the past two weeks had beaten him to the border and gotten away clean.

He could have gone on across the border too, Longarm thought as he waited for his food to arrive. It wouldn't have been the first time he'd bent a rule or two in pursuit of a fugitive. Malcolm Barnes wasn't a killer, though, just a skillful con man and counterfeit artist. Longarm had been willing to chase him clear to hell and gone across Colorado, New Mexico, and Arizona because that was his job, but damned if he was going to risk an international incident over somebody like Barnes.

Maybe the fella would go down there south of the border and start printing up phony Mexican money. Then he'd be the *federales'* problem. That would be just fine. Billy Vail might get worked up over Barnes's escape, but not Longarm.

The waitress came out of the kitchen, expertly balancing two heavily laden platters of food. The grin spread across Longarm's face again as she came to the table.

She lowered the full plates to the table and said, "Old Claude out there in the kitchen says that if you stay around

4

town for a while, maybe he can pay off what he still owes on this place, Mister . . . ?''

"Long, Custis Long." He didn't see any harm in providing his name, but he didn't say anything about being a deputy United States marshal operating out of the office in Denver.

"Well, Mr. Long, I hope you enjoy your food. I'll go get that coffee for you." She started to turn away, then hesitated and added, "You are able to pay for all this, aren't you?"

Longarm didn't take offense. His gun and his boots were well cared for, but other than that he looked pretty rundown. He dug in his shirt pocket, brought out a ten-dollar gold piece, and placed it on the table. "If I eat my way through all of that, I'll be surprised."

The waitress looked at the heaps of food on the plates and raised one eyebrow. "I'm not sure I will be."

The instinctive liking Longarm felt for her grew even more. It wasn't just that she was pretty and he had been on the trail for quite a while without even a glimpse of the fairer sex. He liked her sense of humor and the intelligence in her green eyes every bit as much as the way her breasts pushed against the front of that gray dress—although he had to admit that her breasts *were* right perky.

He dug into the food while she filled a coffee cup and brought it over to the table. Much as he had enjoyed the mild flirting so far, he was too busy for it now. The steak was pretty tough, which came as no surprise, but he had strong teeth. The potatoes were good, just peppery enough, the biscuits were light and fluffy, and the flapjacks swimming in molasses were some of the best Longarm had ever tasted. Old Claude was a hell of a cook, he concluded.

The waitress had other customers to tend to, but she managed to show up at his table with the coffeepot every time his cup got empty. He noticed her watching him from time to time too, whenever she had a chance. Her gaze was frankly interested without being too bold.

Longarm asked for another stack of flapjacks, and by the time he finished them, he was pleasantly full. He leaned back in the chair, sipped his coffee, and sighed.

5

The waitress came over to the table again and surprised him by sitting down opposite him. She said, "I like to see a man enjoy good food, and you've been downright entertaining this morning, Mr. Long." She stuck her hand out toward him. "I'm Faye McCormick."

Longarm took her hand, which was about the coolest thing he had touched in Inferno. "Mighty pleased to meet you, Mrs. McCormick." There was no ring on her hand, but a lady who worked in a hash house might take it off while she was busy waitressing.

"It is Mrs. McCormick," she confirmed, then added, "I'm a widow."

"Sorry to hear that, ma'am," Longarm murmured, and meant it. At least a little. Faye McCormick looked a mite young to be a widow, but out here on the frontier, plenty of gals had buried a husband—or two—before they ever reached twenty years old.

"My husband and I were on our way to California from Georgia when he caught a fever and died," said Faye. "Going to California was Nelson's dream, not mine, so I decided to stay on here and work for a while before I go back home. That was last year. I'm still here."

"Yes, ma'am, I can see that," Longarm said mildly. He didn't recall asking Faye to tell him her life story, but he was generally polite whenever a pretty young woman decided to talk to him. She was probably one of those folks who were just naturally open about things.

"We sold our farm before we started west. I've been saving the money I make here so that maybe I can buy it back. Although I'm not sure why I'd want to. I never liked farming that much."

"If you save up enough money, you can go anywhere you want, do just about anything you like," Longarm told her. "Nothing says you have to go back."

"You know, that's true." She smiled across the table at him. "My goodness, Mr. Long, you're the first person I've talked to about this, and you've given me some fine advice. I hope you don't think I'm too forward."

"No, ma'am, not at all."

"It's just that there's something about you that makes it easy to talk to you."

Maybe it was the interrogation skills he had learned from his years as a lawman, he thought to himself. Or maybe Inferno was just such a small place that Faye McCormick was desperate to talk to somebody who came from somewhere else.

He slid one of his last cheroots from the pocket of his shirt and stuck it in his mouth. He planned to catch the next eastbound train through here, but before he did, he would have to see if the emporium carried cheroots so that he could stock up on them again. He could do without the things if he had to, but he preferred not to.

With a scrape of chair legs on the plank floor, Longarm slid his chair back and started to stand up. "It's been mighty nice talking to you, Miz McCormick," he began, "but I reckon I'd better be—"

That was when the door of the cafe slammed open and three men sauntered in like they owned the place.

Longarm glanced at them, not much liking the looks of them. Young cowboys, probably off one of the spreads to the north. Gun-hung, thumbs hooked in their belts, a slightly unsteady arrogance to their stance that told him they had probably been drinking all night. He wouldn't have paid much attention to them if he hadn't looked at Faye and seen the worried frown on her face.

"Something wrong?" he asked quietly as he lowered himself back into his chair.

Before she had a chance to reply, the bleary eyes of one of the newcomers lit on the table and the two people seated at it. "Faye!" the cowboy bellowed. "There you are! I been lookin' all over town for you, darlin'."

"You know I'm working here every day at this time, Davey," she said tightly to him as he started across the room toward the table. His two cronies followed. Faye looked down at the table as the three of them stopped beside it.

The one called Davey looked owl-eyed at Longarm, then suddenly slapped a palm down on the tabletop, making Faye

7

flinch. "Who the hell's this?" demanded Davey, gesturing at Longarm with his other hand. "This bastard botherin' you, Faye?"

Longarm's teeth clamped a little tighter on the unlit cheroot in his mouth, but he didn't say anything, didn't move. He just looked blandly up at Davey.

But inside he was mad as hell. The breakfast and the conversation with Faye had just started to make him feel better, and now this proddy cowboy and his pards had to come stumbling in and ruin it. Davey was looking for a fight. That much was obvious to Longarm. It was equally clear that he regarded Faye as his girl.

He said as much, glowering at Longarm as he went on. "I don't cotton to no saddle tramp comin' in here and makin' eyes at her neither."

Longarm took the cheroot out of his mouth, using his left hand just in case. "Listen, old son," he said, "I'm not looking for any trouble—"

"Well, you've sure as hell got some!"

"—I just wanted a good breakfast," Longarm went on as if he hadn't heard Davey's last heated statement. "Miz McCormick served the food; that's her job here, in case you didn't know. And then she was polite enough to pass the time of day with a weary stranger. That's all."

Davey hit Longarm hard in the shoulder with the heel of his hand. "Get up!" he said. "On your feet, you saddle tramp bastard! I'll teach you to mess with my gal!"

This was ludicrous, Longarm thought. He had been in this situation more than once, unfortunately, and every time he had regarded the whole thing as downright stupid. And yet he couldn't ignore Davey, as that was liable to just make things worse. Nor could he take the young man too lightly. Davey might be a few boxcars short of a full train and drunk to boot, but that didn't mean he wasn't dangerous. A man was just as dead whether he was killed by a sober scholar or a boozed-up halfwit.

Longarm started to get to his feet, still hoping he could head off trouble. "Why don't you and your pards walk over to the saloon with me?" he suggested to Davey. "I'd be right pleased to buy you a drink.'' Maybe that would be enough to make all three of them pass out, he added to himself.

"I wouldn't drink with the likes of you,'' snarled Davey.

Faye spoke up again, saying, "Please, Davey, don't do this again—''

"Shut up!'' The young cowboy's hand flashed toward her face as she shrank back in her chair. Another instant and his palm would have cracked across her cheek in a vicious slap.

His hand never got there. Fingers like iron clamped painfully around his wrist, jerking it to a halt, and he looked up with a surprised sneer into the face of the stranger who had moved like lightning.

Longarm said quietly, "You don't know how much I wish you hadn't tried to do that, old son.''

Chapter 2

After that moment's startled pause, Davey recovered his wits—so to speak—and gave a wild yell as he flung a punch at Longarm's head. Longarm ducked easily under the round-house blow and used his free hand to hook a hard punch into Davey's midsection. Breath laden with the sour fumes of rotgut whiskey gushed from the cowboy's mouth into Longarm's face.

With a grimace, Longarm shoved Davey away from him. Davey ran into one of his friends, blocking that hombre momentarily, but the third cowboy was already leaping toward Longarm with an angry shout.

Faye came up out of her chair and cried, "Not in here! Please, don't fight in here!"

It was much too late for such an entreaty to do any good. A brawl was just about the last thing Longarm had wanted, but now that one had started, he had no choice but to defend himself. He blocked a punch thrown by the third cowboy and slammed a hard right into the man's mouth. The cowboy rocked back, blood welling from his pulped lips. He gave a strangled grunt of pain.

Davey had caught his balance by now, and he and the second cowboy both lunged at Longarm. He tried to twist away from them, but the other man caught hold of his arm and slowed him down. That gave Davey the chance to club a fist against the side of Longarm's head. The lawman's Stetson went flying.

Longarm stumbled a little as the second cowboy yanked hard on his arm. His booted feet thudded hard against the plank floor as he caught his balance and set himself to fight back. He dealt first with the man who had grabbed him. A short uppercut to the chin jerked the man's head back and loosened his grip. Longarm stepped in and lifted his knee into the cowboy's groin, and that put the puncher out of the fight for the moment. The fella let go of Longarm and clutched himself instead, howling and doubling over.

Longarm pivoted and ducked to let another of Davey's wild punches sail harmlessly over his head. He bent a little more at the knees, reached out and caught Davey around the thighs, and straightened. With a heave, he sent the cowboy flying backward to land with a crash that shook the floor.

So far the fight hadn't done any damage to their surroundings, but that might not continue to hold true. From the corner of his eye, Longarm saw that some of the customers had fled, while others had gotten out of the way to watch the fracas. Faye stood to one side looking scared and worried, and she had been joined by an old man in a long white apron, probably Claude from the kitchen, the owner of the place. Longarm hoped for their sake that the cafe didn't get busted up too much.

Unfortunately, he had to worry about something getting busted besides tables and chairs—such as his head. The cowboy with the bloody mouth came plowing in again, his arms windmilling. Longarm couldn't hope to block every one of the flurry of punches, and sure enough, a knobby-knuckled fist cracked against his jaw a moment later, staggering him. Davey, who had climbed groggily back onto his feet, lunged at Longarm with an incoherent yell and managed to pin both of his arms. That gave Bloody Mouth the opportunity to step in and start slugging punches into Longarm's stomach.

After the big breakfast Longarm had eaten, it took only a couple of the brutal blows to send a wave of nausea rolling

12

through him. He had waited too damned long for that food only to lose it again this soon, so he lifted his right foot and planted the heel of his boot in Bloody Mouth's chest. A hard shove sent the cowboy backward, his arms flailing helplessly, and Longarm and Davey went staggering in the other direction. Bloody Mouth landed on one of the tables. It collapsed under him with a splintering of wood and the crash of crockery.

Longarm tore free of Davey's grip and whirled around to land a haymaker on the young cowboy's jaw. Davey's eyes rolled up in his head and glazed over as consciousness deserted him. His knees unhinged and he fell to the floor, out cold.

Bloody Mouth was more than half-stunned too. He sprawled in the wreckage of the busted table and moaned, all the fight gone out of him. That left only the second man, the one Longarm had kneed in the balls.

The one who was now on his feet again, Longarm saw as he turned around. The cowboy was still clutching himself with his left hand, but his right was leveling a pistol straight at Longarm.

Faye yelped, "Mr. Long, look out!" but the warning wasn't necessary. Longarm had already seen that the pistol being pointed at him by the cowboy was an old single-action Walker Colt and in the man's drunken rage, he had forgotten to cock the blasted thing. He could stand there and pull the trigger of the ancient thumb-buster until the cows came home, but it wasn't going to accomplish a damned thing.

Still, he might figure out sooner or later that all he needed to do was ear back the revolver's hammer. Longarm didn't intend to give him that much time. It was unnerving having that big-bored Walker staring at him, whether it would fire or not. Palming his own Colt from the cross-draw rig, Longarm sprang forward and lashed out with the gun.

The barrel cracked first across the startled cowboy's wrist, making him screech in pain and drop the heavy pistol. Then Longarm backhanded the man, still holding his revolver. The Colt slammed into the cowboy's jaw, the sight tearing a gash in his skin as it did so. He fell back and to the side, moaning incoherently as he slumped to the floor.

Longarm was breathing a little hard. It wasn't easy fighting on a full stomach. A glance around the room told him that all three of his opponents were either unconscious or at least no longer a threat, so he holstered his Colt.

Faye hurried over to him and caught hold of his left arm. "Are you all right, Mr. Long?" she asked anxiously.

Longarm nodded. "I reckon. I'm sure sorry about all this." He inclined his head toward the sprawled figures of Davey and the other two cowboys to indicate what he meant.

Claude—if that was who the old man in the apron was— came across the room and said, "It wasn't your fault, mister. Faye told me how Davey and them friends of his started it. I reckon you was just defendin' yourself."

"And me," Faye put in.

"I'm sorry about the damage anyway," said Longarm. He bent over Davey's recumbent form and slid some fingers into the cowboy's shirt pocket. When his hand emerged, he was holding a double eagle. Straightening, Longarm grinned and went on. "You're lucky he didn't drink this up already. It ought to cover the cost of what got broken." He handed the gold piece to Claude.

The old man seemed reluctant to take the coin, but after a couple of seconds he did. "Much obliged," he said, "and no offense, mister, but you better get out of here while you still can."

Longarm frowned. "What do you mean? These fellas likely to have friends who wouldn't take kindly to them getting whipped?"

"It ain't that," Claude began.

Faye's grip on Longarm's arm tightened. "Somebody's liable to have gone looking for the sheriff to tell him about the fight. Sheriff Thurgood will send some deputies down here."

Longarm shrugged his broad shoulders. "That's all right. The other boys started the fracas, not me."

Moving closer to him, Faye let an undertone of urgency creep into her voice as she said, "You don't understand,

Mr. Long. Take our word for it, it would be better if you weren't around when the deputies got here.''

A frown dug furrows in Longarm's forehead. Suddenly, he had a feeling there was more wrong in this town than just some drunken cowboys on the prod.

But it wasn't really any of his business, and besides, he didn't intend to stay in Inferno for very long. He was already overdue back in Denver, so he didn't need anything else to delay him.

Claude helped him make up his mind by saying to Faye, "You get on out o' here too, honey. When Davey wakes up, he's likely to tell things different than they really happened, and I'd rather you wasn't around while he's feelin' so mean." The old man looked at Longarm. "If you could see that Faye gets back to her place all right, mister, I'd take it kindly."

Longarm hesitated only a moment longer, then nodded. Faye tugged lightly on his arm and said, "We can go out the back."

He scooped up his Stetson from the floor, then let her lead him through the kitchen and out the rear door of the cafe building. Longarm felt a little uneasy about leaving Claude behind to explain everything to the law, especially if Davey was liable to paint the fracas in a different light once he woke up. But Faye and Claude both seemed to know what they were doing, and they definitely wanted Longarm out of there. They knew their town better than he did, so he wasn't going to argue. Besides, there had been other witnesses, and surely they would support Claude in telling the law what had really happened.

Longarm and Faye made their way along the backs of the buildings toward the western edge of the settlement. Longarm heard some shouting from the street, but no one bothered them or tried to stop them. When they reached the outskirts of Inferno, he saw several small houses scattered around, some of them apparently abandoned. If the inhabitants of Inferno weren't careful, the town was liable to dry up and blow away, he thought. Faye headed straight for one of the houses that wasn't deserted. In fact, it was the most

15

neatly kept of all, and it sported a fresh coat of whitewash.

Longarm commented on that, and Faye said, "I like a place to look good. Back on the farm, I swept the floor in the cabin three times a day."

"And it was a dirt floor," Longarm guessed.

She shot a grin at him. "That's right." She seemed calmer, less frightened now. "You can stay here with me today, then get your horse and slip out of town tonight."

Again, Longarm had the sensation that something was badly wrong around here. Why would a man who was in the right in a dispute have to slip out of town under cover of darkness? He didn't explain to her that he had intended to remain in Inferno until the next eastbound train came through. Now he wasn't so sure about that.

"I was riding most of the night," he said. "Once I'd gotten some breakfast, I planned to sleep for a good long while."

"I've got a bed," Faye said as she opened the door of the house.

There was more than one way a fella could take a statement like that, Longarm thought as he followed her into the house. It was dim inside, and the thick adobe walls made the air a little cooler. Faye shut the door behind Longarm.

He took his Stetson off and slapped it against his leg, causing dust to rise from both the hat and his denim trousers. "I surely do appreciate the offer, ma'am," he said, "but there's no way I can crawl into a lady's bed and dirty up her sheets with all this trail dust, especially when the lady keeps as neat a house as you do."

"Well, just take those clothes off," she said. "There's a basin and a pitcher of water in the bedroom. You can wash up before you go to sleep. I'll wash those clothes for you."

"I couldn't ask you to—"

"You didn't," she said with a smile. "I volunteered."

That was true enough, Longarm supposed. And now that the extra boost of energy he'd gotten from the fight with the three cowboys was wearing off, weariness was setting in again. "I sure won't argue with you," he said to Faye.

"And I appreciate everything you've done for me, more than you can know."

"It was worth any trouble to see the look on Davey's face when you grabbed his wrist. He's been getting his way for so long around here . . ." She stopped short, but not before Longarm heard the anger and frustration in her voice.

"That fella's slapped you around before, hasn't he?" Longarm asked quietly.

Faye shrugged and didn't meet his eyes. "Not just me. The girls who work in the saloons all know not to cross him. And it's not just women either."

"Sort of runs roughshod over the whole town, does he?"

Faye put a hand on his arm. "Now don't you go thinking about mixing into this, Mr. Long. You'll just wind up getting yourself hurt, and you'll cause more trouble for the rest of us. You don't want that, do you?"

"No, I surely don't," Longarm replied honestly. He left it at that.

But he wasn't convinced that he and Davey had seen the last of each other.

Whatever he did, it could wait until later, after he'd had some rest. Faye showed him the small bedroom. There was a basin and a pitcher of tepid water on the bureau, just as she had promised. When she had left the room and closed the door behind her, Longarm stripped his shirt off, then removed his boots and the dusty jeans, tossing them and the shirt into a pile by the door. Standing there in his socks and the bottom half of a pair of summerweight long underwear, he poured some water into the basin, dipped a cloth in it, and started swabbing the accumulated grime of the long, fruitless pursuit from his skin.

The door opened again, and Faye took a step into the room before she stopped short and uttered softly, "Oh! I didn't mean to . . ."

The hell she didn't, Longarm thought. She was way too smart to have forgotten so quickly that she had just told him to take his clothes off not two minutes before she came blundering back in here. She didn't scream and hide her eyes, though, so Longarm didn't see any point in getting upset either. He had half-turned when she opened the door, so she had a good view of his broad chest with its mat of curly, dark brown hair. For a long moment they stood there looking at each other, and during that time, Faye's gaze wandered a considerable distance south of his chest. Longarm was aware of how the long underwear was clinging to him. So was Faye.

"Oh, my," she said eventually. "I hope I haven't embarrassed you, Mr. Long."

He smiled. "Seeing as how I'm standing here in my long underwear, ma'am, it might be best if you were to call me Custis."

"All right . . . Custis. I just came in to tell you to put your dirty clothes by the door, but I see you've already done it. I didn't think you would have, ah, disrobed already."

Longarm wasn't sure whether to believe that or not, but if she wanted to, that was fine with him. A respectable widow lady like Mrs. McCormick might not want to admit, even to herself, that she had been hoping for a glimpse of a male visitor in his underwear—or less.

"That's all right," Longarm told her. Under other circumstances, he might have invited her to stay a while, but he was tired. Truly tired. All he really wanted was to finish washing up, then crawl between those crisp white sheets on the bed and pound his ear against those pillows for a few hours.

Faye tore her eyes away from him and bent to pick up the pants and shirt. "I'll wash these and hang them on the line for you," she said. "In this heat, it won't take long for them to dry."

"I appreciate it, ma'am."

Her smile was sly as she echoed what he had said earlier. "Seeing as how you're standing there in your long underwear, Custis, don't you think you ought to call me Faye?"

"Yes, ma'am . . . Faye."

Still smiling, she turned away and went out of the room, taking the dirty clothes with her. She shut the door softly behind her.

Longarm grinned and resumed what he had been doing before she pleasantly interrupted him. It had been entertaining as all hell to stand there and trade witty repartee with the young and pretty Widow McCormick, but he had something else in mind right now.

Five minutes later he was snoring quietly in Faye's bed, deep in slumber.

Chapter 3

Longarm had no idea what time it was when he woke up. He didn't open his eyes to see how light it was in the room. Instead he just lay there dozing, reveling at the feeling of being well rested for the first time in days, maybe weeks.

It didn't take long for a few worries to start creeping into his drowsy brain, however. He recalled the fight he'd had with Davey and the other two cowboys. By itself, a scuffle like that didn't mean a whole hell of a lot. Some fellas got drunk, blew off some steam by starting a fight, then got more than they intended when they picked the wrong gent to hooraw. It happened a lot in these little frontier towns . . . only usually the bullies didn't wind up getting whipped by their intended victim.

What really bothered Longarm was the reaction of Faye and Claude after the fight was over. They had acted like the real trouble had yet to begin.

Longarm had seen other towns that wound up under the thumbs of some would-be badmen. He didn't know anything about the local authorities. Could be that Sheriff Thurgood he'd heard mentioned was just as cowed by Davey and the other two cowboys as Faye and Claude and the rest of the citizens seemed to be.

Would the law take it out on Claude just because the fight had started in his place? Would Faye get blamed as well?

Longarm wouldn't stand for that. He would stay in Inferno long enough to make sure everything got straightened out properly, even if meant missing the next train and getting back to Denver that much later.

Those thoughts brought him fully awake, and he shifted a little in the bed, intending to swing his feet out from under the covers and sit up. But as he moved, something rolled against his back.

Something warm and soft . . . and female.

Longarm's eyes snapped wide open. Whoever was in bed with him—and he had no doubt it was Faye McCormick—snuggled closer against him and muttered sleepily. Longarm couldn't make out what she said, if indeed it made any sense at all.

Now that his eyes were open, he could see bright sunshine around the edges of the curtains that Faye had drawn closed over the room's single window. It was midday at least, maybe a little later. He hadn't been asleep more than a few hours, but he felt refreshed anyway.

Under the circumstances, he doubted if he could doze off again any time soon, even if he wanted to.

Faye seemed to be naked. He could feel her breasts pressed against his back. When she shifted her hips a little, he thought he felt the nap of hair at the juncture of her thighs rubbing against his rump through the thin fabric of the long underwear. Her breath was hot against his left shoulder blade.

He took a deep breath, unsure what to do next. The way she was cuddled against him felt mighty nice . . . so nice that he wanted to roll over and show her just how much he liked it. But evidently, she was asleep, and he didn't want to disturb her. Her job at the cafe might require her to get up long before dawn, maybe as early as four o'clock in the morning. She was probably tired. That was why she had crawled in here beside him. And a lady couldn't be held responsible for anything she might do in her sleep, especially a widow lady who had been accustomed in the past to having a male body beside her in the bed.

22

Then he felt the touch of her hand on his hip, moving so lightly that he wasn't sure at first if he was imagining it. Her fingertips danced over his skin just above the waistband of his long underwear and explored on around his body, playing over his hard, flat belly. The frequency of her breath against his back seemed to have increased a mite, he thought.

The pace of his own breathing had sure picked up, and it began to gallop as she slid her hand underneath his underwear. His shaft had started to stiffen as soon as he felt her pressed against him, and the sensation of her smooth, cool fingers wrapping themselves around it made him come to a full erection. So full, in fact, that it was a little uncomfortable, trapped in the tight confines of the long underwear.

She gasped as she felt the length and heft of him, and he knew she was awake. A moment later she whispered, ''Lift your hips.'' He was glad to do so. She pushed the underwear down so that his organ sprang free.

Faye began to pump her tightly gripping hand up and down. As she did so, she raised her body a little so that she could plant a kiss on the back of his neck. Her fingers might be cool, but her mouth was burning hot, Longarm discovered. She kept kissing him, her lips and tongue blazing a trail down his back, between his shoulder blades.

Longarm's hips moved back and forth involuntarily as she caressed him. He didn't want this ending too soon, so when he started to shiver and throb, he reached down and grasped her hand, pulling it away from him. She made a little noise of disappointment.

He didn't want her to feel let down, so he rolled over quickly, bringing him face-to-face with her. Faye's chestnut hair hung around her lovely features as she brought her mouth to his with a breathless urgency. Her tongue slipped into his mouth, a hot and wet visitor that was more than welcome. His own tongue met it eagerly.

At the same time, he reached down and cupped her breasts, each of them a generous handful. The nipples were hard as little pebbles, and he rubbed his thumbs over them gently. She thrust her hips at him, and his shaft slipped between her thighs to rub against the buttery heat of her core without penetrating it. Her lightly furred triangle pushed almost desperately at his groin.

Longarm could have taken her easily then, rolled on top and filled her hot, wet needing. She was nearly frantic with want. But it had been a long time for both of them, obviously, and he wanted it to be special. He threw back the sheet so that he could look at her in the dim light that filled the room. She was beautifully, wantonly naked. She moved onto her back and opened her thighs, spreading them invitingly.

Always the gentleman, Longarm accepted the invitation, although not in the way she expected. He twisted around and brought his mouth to her core, tickling the insides of her thighs with his longhorn mustache and spreading her open even more with his fingers before he plunged his tongue into her.

Faye screamed.

It was a low, breathy sound, however, despite its intensity, and Longarm doubted it would carry beyond the thick adobe walls of the house. Her thighs clamped spasmodically on his ears as she kept gasping. She acted like a woman who had never had a fella give her French lessons before. If that was the case, her late husband had sure missed out on an appealing prospect.

Faye might not have ever been on the receiving end, but she knew all about giving, Longarm discovered a moment later. The way he was turned around, it was easy for her to reach out, grasp his pole with both hands, and close her mouth over the tip of it. She moved her hands and lips down, swallowing more and more of him as he continued what he was doing between her clutching thighs. She shook and shuddered and moaned in her throat, but she hung on tight.

Neither one of them could last much longer, Longarm sensed. After a few dizzying moments that seemed like an eternity, he lifted his head and eased himself back around so that he was kneeling between her legs. They were both so wet that entering her was simplicity itself. He just gave a little thrust of his hips and he was in her, sunk to the hilt, filling her to the brim. She cried out again.

There was no time to waste now. Longarm pounded into her, reaching depths even he might have thought impossible. They were no longer two beings. They were one, united in passion and need. Faye wrapped her arms around him and held him tightly to her as he pumped in and out of her. Finally he drove even deeper, stiffened, and held there as his climax came boiling out of him. It seemed as if it would never end, an infinite flood of heat that washed over both of them and swept them away.

But end it did, and Longarm caught himself on his elbows to keep himself from crushing her with his weight as he drew in great heaving breaths of air. Faye was panting with exertion too, and a fine sheen of sweat covered both of their bodies.

"It's really too . . . hot to be doing this," Faye finally said. "We could come down with . . . heatstroke."

"I reckon you're right," said Longarm. He rolled to the side and sprawled next to her on the damp sheet. "If a fella's going to get all sweaty, though . . . that's the way to do it."

She tipped her head back against the pillow and laughed, a clear, musical sound. She was too fine to be stuck in a heat-baked, backwater town like Inferno, Longarm thought. But she stayed here of her own free choice, and it wasn't his place to disparage her decision.

Still, he couldn't help but think of how she would look in the parlor of a fine house in Denver.

With a sigh, she rested her head against his shoulder. "I hope you won't think I'm too shameless," she said without looking up at him. "It's been such a long time since Nelson died."

"You don't have to say any more," Longarm told her. "I think mighty high of you."

"Some people would say that I was dishonoring his memory."

"Did the two of you love each other?"

That question brought her head up so that she could meet

his eyes. "Yes," she said solemnly. "Yes, we did."

"Then he'd want you to be happy," said Longarm, equally serious.

"I am," she whispered. "Right now, I'm so very happy."

"Then I don't reckon ol' Nelson would ever hold that against you. And nobody else should either."

Faye smiled. "You are some man, Mr. Custis Long. Some man . . ."

He might have thanked her for the compliment if he'd had the time.

But the next instant, there was a crash from the other room as somebody kicked the front door of the house open.

Instinctively recognizing the sound for what it was, Longarm rolled out of bed and lunged toward the bureau, where he had placed his holstered Colt and the coiled shell belt. Before he could reach the gun, the door of the bedroom slammed open as well, and a harsh voice yelled, "Freeze, mister, or I'll blow that naked ass o' yours clean off!"

Longarm had no choice but to stop his reaching motion while he was still a foot short of the Colt's walnut grips. He looked over his shoulder and saw three men crowding into the room. All of them had pistols drawn and leveled at him. Faye screamed and jerked the sheet up over her nakedness.

"Well, well, well," said the man who had shouted the command to freeze at Longarm. He was a little below medium height, and his weasel-like features had been cured by the sun to the color of saddle leather. "Ain't this cozy?" he went on with a leer. "The saddle tramp's screwin' the Widow McCormick, just like the sheriff figured."

Longarm had already noticed that all three of the unwanted visitors were wearing tin stars. The reference to the sheriff confirmed his guess that they were deputies. But they weren't acting very professionally in the performance of their duties. They were too busy trying to get a glimpse of Faye's naked body under that sheet.

"You boys are making a mistake," Longarm said. "Why don't you go out into the other room, and I'll get dressed. We can hash all this out in a minute or two."

The apparent leader of the trio shook his head. "Nope, we got our orders. We come to take you into custody, Long, and we ain't lettin' you out of our sight. If you want to get dressed, you just go right ahead." He grinned at Faye. "You too, if you want, ma'am."

She just clutched the thin sheet tighter around her. "I'll do no such thing!" she snapped. "You get out of here, Clark. Don't you have any shame?"

"No, ma'am, I guess not. But I got a job to do, and that's arrestin' this saddle tramp here."

Longarm straightened from his crouch, then moving slowly and carefully so as not to spook the three badge-toters, he picked up the long underwear from the floor where it had wound up and stepped into it. "My pants and shirt are over there," he said, pointing to the pile of dirty clothes just inside the door.

The deputy called Clark kicked the garments over to him. He wished he had been wearing his vest despite the heat, because that was where the little derringer he usually carried was hidden. There were no weapons in the pants and shirt except a folding knife in the pocket of the jeans.

Longarm pulled the clothes on, repeating as he did so, "This is all a mistake. What are the charges against me?"

"Assault, attempted murder, and disturbin' the peace," replied Clark without hesitation. "You busted up Davey and his pards pretty good. They'll be laid up for a couple of weeks, maybe longer. Can't have strangers beatin' up our good citizens."

"Good citizens!" Faye repeated in indignation. "Mr. Long didn't do anything except try to defend himself—and me! Davey was about to slap me!"

"That ain't the way we heard the story," Clark declared. "The witnesses all say Davey and his friends were mindin' their own business when this fella jumped 'em for no reason. But he can tell his side of it to Judge Schofield, I reckon."

Longarm felt a sinking sensation in his middle. The fear he had sensed in this town had evidently influenced the way the witnesses in the cafe had testified. Everybody was too afraid of Davey to tell what had really happened. Longarm had to hope Sheriff Thurgood and Judge Schofield were honest, reasonable men. If they were, then the U.S. marshal's badge and the identification papers in his saddlebags would go a long way toward convincing them he was telling the truth.

He pulled his socks on and stomped into his boots, then reached for his hat and said, "All right, let's go see the judge."

Before he could pick up the Stetson, one of the other deputies yelled, "Look out! He's got a gun hid under there!"

Longarm's guts turned cold as the implication of the words flashed through his mind. They were going to shoot him down and claim he had resisted arrest. They might even plant a pistol under his hat just to support their story. He had to move fast or die right here and now.

He lunged away from the bureau, going straight at the deputies rather than away from them, as they must have expected. Before the startled Clark could pull the trigger of his gun, Longarm barreled into him and drove him back into the other two star-packers. Longarm reached out and grabbed the cylinder of one of the guns, preventing it from turning so that it wouldn't fire. At the same time he lifted the elbow of his other arm into the chin of the third deputy, driving the man's head back. Clark was still struggling to regain his balance when Longarm kicked him in the stomach.

Faye was screaming again. Longarm didn't want any gunplay in this little room, because the likelihood was high that a stray shot would strike Faye. He snapped a punch into the face of the man whose gun he had hold of, then jerked the weapon free and tossed it behind him.

Lowering his head, Longarm drove forward and butted the deputy just below the sternum. He wrapped his arms around the fellow's waist and hung on as his legs continued churning. The deputy went backward with a startled yell and crashed into the other two. All three of them went down. Longarm was the only one remaining on his feet.

He stepped back quickly, intending to snatch up the gun he had tossed aside and cover the three of them, but as he moved Clark had the presence of mind to hook a booted toe behind Longarm's left ankle. Longarm felt his balance deserting him. He grabbed at the bureau to hold himself up but missed. With bone-jarring force, his backside landed on the floor.

Clark scrambled up, his pointed features contorted with rage. He threw himself on top of Longarm, and the hand still holding his gun rose and fell viciously. The barrel of the revolver thudded against Longarm's head. Pain exploded through the marshal's skull.

Longarm tried to throw Clark off, but he was too stunned. Clark lifted the gun, ready to continue the pistol-whipping, but before the second blow could fall, Faye leaped out of bed, her nakedness forgotten, and grabbed the deputy's arm. "No!" she cried.

The other two men were pulling themselves to their feet, and the sight of the naked young beauty struggling with their partner made them pause for a second. Then one of the deputies grabbed her, grinning hugely as he wrapped his arms around her. "I got her, Clark!" he exclaimed.

Blackness dotted with red stars was closing in around Longarm. He heard Faye cry out again, and that gave him the strength to fling a punch at Clark's face. The deputy jerked aside so that the blow only grazed his head, however, and then he clubbed Longarm again with the gun. "One of you hang on to that hellcat!" he shouted. "The other one give me a hand with this drifter!"

Clark wasn't going to need much help. Longarm was barely hanging on to consciousness, and as he heard Faye struggling and shrieking, the last of his senses slipped away from him.

He was sinking in a vast, dark nothingness, settling lower and lower until he was completely gone.

Chapter 4

The good thing about hurting so bad, Longarm supposed, was that the pain assured him he was still alive. He wasn't sure what lay on the other side of the grave; he had always agreed with the message of the old hymn about knowing more about it farther along. But he was pretty damned sure that a dead man wouldn't have such a hellacious headache.

As more of his senses seeped back into his awareness, he realized he was lying on his back on something hard and flat. His right arm was dangling limply to the side. He moved his hand a little, and felt his fingertips brush what felt like a rough stone floor.

Longarm sighed. Like it or not, he was going to have to pry his eyes open and see where he was . . . although he figured he could make a pretty good guess.

Slowly, he lifted his eyelids, blinking a couple of times as light struck his eyes. The light had patterns of shadow in it, confusing Longarm for a moment until he realized the shadows were cast by the bars in the window on the other side of the cell. He could see it when he turned his head a little, wincing as he did so.

Yep, he was in jail, all right.

He pushed himself up on his elbows and shook his head, then regretted it mightily. When the world settled down again after a few seconds, he was able to swing his legs over the side of the narrow cot where he lay. With a groan, he sat up and steadied his head with his hands. There were a couple of sore lumps above his left ear, each of them matted with hair and dried blood.

Longarm cursed through gritted teeth. If he ever got his hands on that pistol-whipping bastard Clark . . .

"So, you're awake, are you?" asked a hoarse voice from the other side of the barred door. "Good. The judge is waitin' for you."

Longarm looked up and saw a powerful-looking man standing in the corridor that led down the center of the cell block. The man had broad shoulders, graying dark hair, and a thin mustache. Pinned on his vest was a more elaborate badge than Longarm had seen earlier on the deputies.

"You'd be Sheriff Thurgood?" Longarm forced the words out, even though his mouth didn't want to work at first.

"That's right. Carl Thurgood, sheriff of this here county. And you're Custis Long." Thurgood's voice sounded like he had been punched in the throat one too many times.

"United States Deputy Marshal Custis Long," declared Longarm angrily. "You've locked up a fellow lawman, Thurgood, on the say-so of a hot-headed, no-account cowboy."

Thurgood shook his head. "I don't know nothin' about you bein' a federal badge, Long. To me, you're just another troublemakin' drifter."

Longarm came to his feet, trying to ignore the wave of unsteadiness that went through him. "I've got identification, damn it!" he said. "Check the saddlebags on that dun I rode into town. My bona fides are in there."

"Your saddlebags, and all the rest of your gear, have been turned over to Judge Schofield as evidence. You can argue with him about it if you're of a mind to." Thurgood chuckled humorlessly. "Don't reckon it'll do you much good, though."

Longarm suppressed a groan. Thurgood struck him as no more honest than he had to be, and the judge was probably the same way. Still, somebody had to see the light of reason sooner or later. Nobody could treat a federal deputy marshal this way for very long without bringing down the wrath of Uncle Sam, Billy Vail, and the United States Justice Department on their heads.

"I'll talk to the judge," said Longarm. "Where is he?"

"Right down the hall," replied Thurgood, reaching for a ring of keys on his belt. He selected one of them, stuck it in the keyhole in the door with his left hand, then stepped back and unholstered a Colt with his right before he turned the key. "Come on out, but don't get any funny ideas. I won't lose a minute's sleep tonight if I have to gun you down, mister."

Longarm knew Thurgood meant it. He went over to the door, pushed it open carefully, and stepped out into the corridor.

The three deputies were waiting in the sheriff's office on the other side of the heavy door that led into the cell block. As soon as Longarm and Thurgood stepped through that door, the sheriff snapped, "Get the irons on him, boys."

Longarm glowered futilely as wrist and ankle shackles were snapped in place on his arms and legs. The irons bit painfully into his flesh, but Clark and the other men didn't seem inclined to loosen them any. Longarm didn't waste any breath asking.

"Move along," ordered Thurgood, stepping close enough behind Longarm to prod him in the back with the six-gun. "Out the door and turn right."

He was in the big stone building that he had noticed on the way into Inferno, Longarm realized. It housed the sheriff's office, the jail, and the local court. Taking short, uncomfortable steps because of the leg irons, he left the office and shuffled down a hallway toward a set of double doors at the end. One of the deputies went ahead to open them.

As Longarm entered the room, followed closely by Sheriff Thurgood and the deputies, he saw the words JUDGE HIRAM SCHOFIELD lettered on one of the doors in gilt paint. Longarm didn't recall ever hearing of the man, which came as no surprise. Until today, he had never heard of Inferno either.

Instead of a typical judge's bench, there was a large table at the front of the room, faced by several rows of straight-backed chairs. Behind the table was a larger, plushly upholstered armchair. It had to be big to hold the man who was sitting there in a black broadcloth suit, white shirt, and black string tie. He would tip the scales at well over two hundred pounds, Longarm thought, but he looked more powerful than fat. Thinning reddish-gray hair was combed over a freckled scalp, and his bushy sideburns trailed down to a short, ginger-colored beard. Judge Schofield had a cigar between his thick lips, and he rolled it from side to side in his mouth as he studied the documents spread out on the table in front of him. Thurgood prodded Longarm up to the other side of the table, opposite the judge.

"Here he is, Your Honor," rasped the sheriff. "You've got the charges against him right there."

"So I do, so I do," said the jurist. He finally looked up at Longarm with watery brown eyes. Around the cigar, he grunted, "I'm Judge Hiram Schofield. Quite the hellraiser, aren't you, my boy?"

Longarm had already spotted his saddlebags lying on the table in front of the judge. He said tightly, "I'm not your boy, Your Honor. I'm Custis Long, U.S. deputy marshal out of the office in Denver. If you'll just look in those saddlebags, you'll find my identification papers."

"Is that so?" Schofield sounded only mildly interested in what Longarm had said. "Well, it may interest you to know, Mr. Long, that I've gone through your belongings already, and I didn't see hide nor hair of any identification papers."

Longarm stiffened, his eyes widening in surprise. "What do you mean they're not there? They have to be!"

Thurgood jammed him in the kidneys with the gun barrel. "Don't talk to the judge that way. Show some respect, Long."

"That's sound advice, Mr. Long," said Schofield. "I could always hold you in contempt of court, you know."

Longarm's jaw tightened, but he didn't say anything. Contempt was what he felt for this court, all right, along with a big helping of anger. It wouldn't do him any good to lose his temper, though. With an effort, he reined it in and said, "If my papers aren't there, somebody must have stolen them."

"Damn it!" exploded Thurgood. "Are you accusin' me and my men of being thieves?"

"Not necessarily," Longarm replied coolly, twisting his head to look at the sheriff. "Where's my horse been since this morning?"

"I had him taken over to the hotel livery stable when you dropped out of sight after that ruckus at the cafe," said Thurgood. "I brought all your gear straight here to the judge, but that's the only time I touched it."

Schofield smiled thinly. "And you don't want to accuse me of theft, Mr. Long. You really don't." The judge opened one of the saddlebags and brought out Longarm's roll of greenbacks. "Besides, if we were thieves, wouldn't we have stolen your money too? There's over a hundred dollars here."

Longarm began, "A hundred and seven dollars—"

"And eighty-nine cents," finished Schofield. "You see, I even counted the money. It's all still here."

"All right," Longarm said grudgingly, "maybe neither of you lifted my papers. But something's happened to them. I'm still a deputy marshal."

Schofield shook his head and spread his hands. "I've seen no proof of that."

Longarm's breath hissed between his teeth in a sigh. He could see that he might as well abandon this line of defense. He said, "I want to answer the charges against me. I fought with those cowboys, but only to defend a lady, then to defend myself." He glanced around the courtroom. Nobody was there except himself, the judge, Sheriff Thurgood, and the deputies. "Where is Mrs. McCormick?"

Schofield took the cigar from his mouth. "Under custody in her home, I suppose you could say, until we get to the bottom of this. Sheriff Thurgood has assigned a deputy to guard the lady's dwelling."

Well, that was something to be thankful for, thought Longarm. At least Faye hadn't been thrown in jail too. He hated to think of what might happen to her in the hands of Clark and the other deputies.

"If you'll ask Mrs. McCormick what happened in the cafe, she'll give you the straight of it," Longarm suggested.

The deputy called Clark snickered. "Looked to me more like *you* was givin' *her* the straight of it when we came into that room, Long!"

Judge Schofield frowned, picked up his gavel, and banged it on the table. "Here now!" he said. "I'll not have that kind of talk in my courtroom, Deputy Clark."

Instantly, the deputy looked apologetic and more than a little frightened. "Sorry, Your Honor," he said quickly. "I didn't mean nothin' by it."

"I want decorum in my courtroom," said Schofield. He turned his attention back to Longarm. "I'm told that Mrs. McCormick interfered with the sheriff's men when they went to her house to arrest you and that she even assaulted one of the deputies! Such a person can't be regarded as a very trustworthy witness, I'd say."

"You're not even going to ask her what happened?" Longarm demanded.

Schofield spread his hands. "I see no point in it."

Longarm's teeth ground together in frustration. He had suspected from the first that this so-called hearing would be a travesty, and he was being proved right with every passing moment. Schofield had no interest in fair and proper procedure.

"Do you have anything else to say in your own behalf, Mr. Long?" asked the judge.

"You don't believe that the fight wasn't my fault?"

"I've heard no testimony to indicate otherwise, except for yours."

"And you don't believe I'm a federal marshal?"

"I've seen no proof of that either." Schofield smiled thinly. "Besides, even if that wild claim is true, it makes no real difference, Mr. Long. Being a federal official gives you no right to break the laws of the Territory of Arizona and this county and town. You're still a citizen just like anyone else, bound by the laws of the land." Clasping his hands together in front of him, Schofield leaned forward, putting some strain on the buttons of his shirt. "Do you have anything else to say?"

Stonily, Longarm shook his head. "I don't reckon it'd do any good."

"Very well, then. It's up to me to render a verdict in this case, and I am prepared to do so." Schofield shoved his chair back from the table and stood up. He was fairly short, and his broad stature made him appear almost as wide as he was tall. Evidently he was in the mood for a little oratory before he announced his verdict. He clasped his hands behind his back and began to pace behind the desk as he said, "You come into our town as a stranger, Mr. Long, and no sooner are you here than you provoke an altercation and attack three of our most upstanding citizens. No amount of recompense on your part can truly relieve the suffering of Davey Bullard, Hoke Jansson, and Lester Dill. These men will be unable to work at their jobs on the Boxed HS Ranch for several weeks, thereby causing great inconvenience for their employer . . . which in this case happens to be me, since I own the Boxed HS."

It was all Longarm could do not to groan. The deck had been stacked against him even more than he knew. No wonder the inhabitants of Inferno gave Davey and his cronies such a free rein to cause trouble. The cowboys rode for Judge Schofield himself, who obviously ruled this part of the country like one of those tin-plated European dictators. Chances were, Sheriff Thurgood and the deputies were all Schofield's handpicked men too. They sure enough hopped when the judge said "frog."

"Therefore," continued Schofield, "I have no choice but to find you guilty of all counts on the charges lodged against you, Mr. Long. I hearby sentence you to pay a fine in the amount of . . . shall we say five thousand dollars?"

Longarm's granite face didn't show any reaction. He had expected Schofield to fine him, rather than sentence him outright to jail time. The amount of the fine didn't really matter, though. Longarm couldn't pay anything more than $107.89—and Schofield knew it.

The judge reached down and picked up the roll of greenbacks from the table. "We'll apply this to your fine, of course, leaving you owing . . . hell, let's round it off. Four thousand eight hundred and ninety-two dollars. Are you prepared to pay, Mr. Long?"

"I can't," Longarm said.

Schofield pretended to be surprised. "What's that? You can't pay the fine against you? Well, well. Something will have to be done about that. The customary procedure is to allow a prisoner to work off a fine if he lacks the funds required to pay in cash. I happen to know of a certain silver mine, over the border in Mexico, where such a debt could be paid." The judge grinned. "I have, ah, an arrangement with the owner of the mine."

Longarm didn't say anything. It was entirely possible, he knew, that Schofield owned the silver mine himself. Longarm had blundered into one of the oldest schemes in the book: a crooked judge and sheriff arresting travelers on trumped-up charges and levying outrageous fines. If the unlucky prisoners had the money to pay the fines, that was all well and good. If they didn't, the judge simply sentenced them to work it off, snagging some virtual slave labor for himself or one of his partners in the process.

Longarm was certain of one thing: If he allowed himself to be taken across the border to that silver mine, he would never get out of the place alive. Schofield, Thurgood, and whoever else was in on the scheme would see to that.

Schofield regarded Longarm coldly across the desk. "Do you have anything to say, Mr. Long?"

What Longarm wanted to do was spit in the fat son of a bitch's eye. He wanted to rail against the injustice of this affair and vow vengeance. He wanted to warn Schofield and Thurgood to just go ahead and kill him now, or otherwise he would be coming after them later. But none of those things would do him a damned bit of good, he knew, so he didn't give in to the impulses. Instead, he said, "Mrs. McCormick was just trying to give me a hand because I helped her earlier. I'd take it kindly if you'd drop any charges against her and let her get on with her life."

"And in return?"

Longarm sighed. "I won't give you or your boys any trouble. I'll do whatever you say." It was an easy lie to tell with Faye's freedom and safety possibly at stake.

Schofield considered for a moment, then nodded. "Of course. I intended to dismiss the charges against Mrs. McCormick anyway. Things happen in the heat of the moment, I'm well aware of that." He looked at Thurgood. "Sheriff, you may remove the guard from Mrs. McCormick's house and inform her that the charges against her have been dropped."

Thurgood nodded. "Sure, Your Honor."

Longarm felt a surge of relief. He wasn't certain why he believed what Schofield had just said, since the judge was obviously as crooked as a sidewinder, but he felt that Schofield and Thurgood would leave Faye alone now. They couldn't afford to arouse the anger of the citizens too much, and that was what might happen if they were too hard on Faye.

The good people of Inferno, though, probably wouldn't give a damn if some stranger was hauled off to a Mexican silver mine as a slave. That had doubtless happened before.

"Take the prisoner back to his cell," ordered Schofield. "Tomorrow he will be taken to the mine, where he will labor until his fine is paid off."

"Yes, sir, Your Honor," husked Thurgood. He took hold of Longarm's shoulder, jerked him around, and shoved him toward the door of the courtroom. "Get movin', Long."

Longarm went, trudging back down the hall toward the jail. But with each short, shuffling step, his anger grew. Schofield, Thurgood, Clark, and all the other crooks mixed up in this scheme were going to be damned sorry he had ever ridden into Inferno. That wasn't bravado, just a fact.

Longarm was already damned sorry he had ridden in.

Chapter 5

The clang of the cell door closing sent an icy shiver down Longarm's spine. He had slammed the bars shut on countless criminals himself, but only on a few occasions had *he* been on the other side—the wrong side—of a cell door. He hadn't liked it before, and he didn't like it now.

"What time is it getting to be?" he asked as Thurgood and the deputies started to leave the cell block. The sheriff turned back and pulled a gold-plated turnip from the watch pocket of his pants.

"Nigh on to three o'clock," said Thurgood. "You weren't unconscious very long after Clark and the boys hauled you in here."

"Why'd you wait until the middle of the day to send somebody after me?" Longarm wasn't sure why he was asking the questions of the crooked sheriff. Maybe he just didn't want to sit here in the cell block all alone.

"Why, we had to do things legal and proper-like," Thurgood said with a grin. "I got statements from all the witnesses who were at the cafe this morning, along with talking to Davey and his pards while the doc was patchin' 'em up. Then I took all the evidence to Judge Schofield, who issued a warrant for your arrest. After that we had to ask around town and see if anybody had seen you. When they hadn't, it didn't take much figurin' to realize you were bedded down with that young woman. Accordin' to everybody we talked to, she took quite a shine to you." He laughed harshly. "If you were really a lawman, the way you claim, you'd know how all this works."

Longarm felt the fires of anger start to flare up inside him again, but he managed to bank the blaze before it got out of control. He purely hated to see somebody like Thurgood hiding behind a facade of law and respectability.

"Those deputies of yours ain't gentlemen. They wouldn't even get out of the room and give Mrs. McCormick a chance to get dressed.'"

"Clark and the boys were just doin' their job," said Thurgood. His grin widened. "They told me how the widow jumped out of bed bare-ass to give you a hand, Long. Clark said that was just about the prettiest sight he'd seen in a month of Sundays."

"They had damned well better not have hurt her," Longarm said heavily.

Thurgood's grin disappeared. "They didn't lay a hand on her," he snapped, " 'cept to keep her from killin' 'em."

"I'm holding you responsible for her safety, Sheriff."

"Fine. Just don't forget you ain't in much of a position to go around threatenin' people."

Longarm changed the subject. "This silver mine you're taking me to over in Mexico . . . Schofield really owns it, doesn't he?"

"Nope," Thurgood answered without hesitation. "The mine belongs to a fella named Don Alfonso Vasquez. Like the judge said, he has a deal with Vasquez to provide prison labor. Vasquez pays fair wages, and the money goes to the town. It's all legal."

Except for the fact that Vasquez's money undoubtedly wound up in the pockets of Schofield, Thurgood, and the deputies, even if it was officially paid to the town. The time it actually spent in Inferno's coffers wouldn't even be enough for it to cool off.

Longarm kept that thought to himself. He was casting around for something else to say when Thurgood rasped, "They don't pay me to stand around jawin' with prisoners."

42

He turned toward the cell block door.

"Wait a minute," said Longarm. "When do you feed people around here? I missed lunch."

"That's because you was too busy puttin' it to the Widow McCormick," Thurgood grunted. "You'll have to wait until supper, round six o'clock."

"That's three hours away!" protested Longarm.

The sheriff just gave him an ugly grin. "Where you're goin', you'd better get used to missin' meals."

Thurgood left the cell block, and Longarm sank down tiredly on the cot. His head still hurt, and he had been telling the truth about being hungry. There was a gnawing ache in his guts, and not all of it came from the bruises he had suffered in the various fights earlier in the day.

Lord, nobody could accuse him of letting grass grow under his feet! he thought. Less than eight hours had passed since he rode into Inferno, and already he had been involved in two major fracases, bedded as sweet a gal as he'd run into in a long time, been knocked out and thrown in jail, and gotten himself a virtual death sentence to some Mexican silver mine.

At this rate, he had to wonder what was going to happen after the sun went down.

The afternoon wore on, and the heat inside the cell rose. Longarm lay back on the cot and sweated. That was about all there was to do. Without meaning to, he dozed off again, and when he woke up, his neck and shoulders and back all ached from the hard surface on which he had slept. The inside of his mouth was dry and tasted like something had crawled in there and died while he was asleep.

He sat up, shook his head in a mostly futile attempt to clear away some of the cobwebs, then got to his feet and walked over to the bars. "Hey!" he called, knowing his voice would penetrate through the iron-barred window in the heavy cell block door. "I'm spittin' cotton in here! How about some water? Anybody out there?"

A moment later he heard the rattle of someone unlocking the cell block door. It swung open, and the deputy called

Clark stepped through. "Hush up your caterwaulin'!" he said. "Ain't no need to yell."

"I'm thirsty," Longarm said. "It's mighty hot back here, and I haven't had any water all afternoon."

"Well, I reckon we can do somethin' about that." Clark disappeared for a moment through the open cell block door, then came back carrying a wooden bucket and a tin dipper. "One of the boys just drew this up from the well a little while ago. It's still nice an' cool."

Just the thought of the water made Longarm's mouth dry up that much more in anticipation. But the nasty grin on Clark's face warned him it wasn't going to be that easy. The deputy scooped water from the bucket with the dipper, then said, "You don't mind drinkin' after me, do you, Long?"

"Go ahead," Longarm said curtly.

Clark drank from the dipper, smacking his lips over the cool water. "Mighty good," he said. "Think I'll have me a little more, then you can have it."

"All right, just hurry it up," said Longarm.

Clark refilled the dipper, took in a big mouthful of the water, then suddenly sprayed it from his mouth at Longarm. Longarm had been expecting something just about that crude from the deputy, so he was able to turn his head and close his eyes, avoiding most of the spray of water and spittle. Clark threw back his head and laughed.

"I told you I'd have it first, then you could have it!" He cackled. "Kept my word, didn't I? Did just what I said!"

"Yeah, it's damned hilarious," Longarm said, making an effort not to lose his temper and goad Clark on that much more. "Can I have the dipper now?"

"Why, that wasn't our deal. I gave you your water, Long, just like you asked for. Now I'm goin' back out there to the office and sit down and smoke me a cigar." Clark pointed at the stone floor inside the cell, where some of the water he had spit out had splashed. There were some rapidly drying wet spots there. "If you're still thirsty, I reckon you can suck up some of what spilled on the floor. Better hurry, though, 'fore it all dries up."

He left the cell block, taking the bucket and dipper with him and laughing his moronic laugh. Longarm spent several pleasurable moments thinking about how good it would feel to slip his fingers around the deputy's scrawny neck and squeeze the life out of him; then he sighed and went back to the cot to sit down.

Wait and sweat, sweat and wait.

For the moment, that just about summed it up.

There was a pleasurable surprise for Longarm as the sun started to slide down the western sky and evening approached. The cell block door opened and Sheriff Thurgood came in. That was neither pleasurable nor a surprise, but what followed him was.

Faye McCormick came into the cell block, carrying a tray with a cloth draped over it.

"Little lady brought you your supper, Long," said Thurgood.

Faye came up to the bars as Longarm stood up. "Are you all right, Custis?" she asked anxiously.

"As all right as I can be, locked up like this," replied Longarm. At the moment, he was more worried about Faye than about himself. He looked her over, checking for bruises or any other sign that she had been hurt, but she seemed to be unharmed. She was wearing a dark blue dress and looked lovely.

"Better step back, Miz McCormick," warned Thurgood. "Can't have you gettin' too close to the prisoner. Jail rules, you know."

Faye flung an angry glance over her shoulder at him. "What's the matter, Sheriff? Are you afraid I'll try to smuggle him a gun or something so that he can get out of this hellhole?"

Thurgood's craggy features hardened, and Longarm wished Faye hadn't said anything. It was too late. She had already antagonized the sheriff.

"Set that tray down over here on the stool," ordered Thurgood.

Faye hesitated. "It's for Mr. Long."

"And you can give it to him in a minute. First, I want to make sure you *ain't* tryin' to smuggle in anything to him."

Longarm's fingers went around the bars and tightened on them. "Leave her alone, Thurgood," he said. "She's not trying to trick anybody."

"Well, now, we don't know that, do we?" Thurgood's voice was even harsher than usual as he went on. "I said bring that tray over here and set it down. Now!"

Faye sighed and moved over to the three-legged stool Thurgood had indicated. She placed the dinner tray on it and then straightened.

"Just stand still," said Thurgood. "I got to make sure you ain't carryin' no weapons."

"Damn it, Thurgood . . ." Longarm began, then lapsed into a seething, enraged silence as Thurgood lifted his hands and placed them on Faye's shoulders. A shudder went through her body, but that was her only reaction as the sheriff moved his hands down slowly over her breasts.

She continued to stand motionless, her face seemingly carved from stone, as he fondled her for several moments. His hands strayed from her breasts down over her belly, then around her hips to the curve of her backside. Thurgood stood close to her, his face etched in tight lines of lust as he kneaded her buttocks. He pressed her stomach against his groin.

Longarm's pulse hammered madly inside his skull. He had never wanted anything more than he wanted to kill Carl Thurgood at that moment. But there was nothing he could do. Thurgood and Faye were both well out of his reach, even if he lunged against the bars and extended his arm as far as it would go.

Finally, Thurgood released Faye and stepped back, grinning broadly. "I don't reckon you're hidin' anything," he said. "Now, just let me check this food you brought over . . ."

"There's a gun in the mashed potatoes and a Bowie knife in the cobbler," Faye said bitterly.

"You're joshin' me," grunted Thurgood. But he picked up the fork on the tray and stabbed it into each dish anyway.

When he was satisfied there was nothing hidden in the food, he handed the tray back to Faye. "All right, go ahead and give it to him."

She took the tray and turned toward Longarm's cell, and as she did so, Thurgood let his hand rest on her rump again, rubbing it back and forth for a second. Then he coughed and said, "I'm, uh, goin' out back for a minute. But don't you try anything, Miz McCormick. There's deputies right out there in the office, and they'll be keepin' an eye on you."

Faye nodded. "Of course, Sheriff."

Thurgood disappeared through the door, and a moment later Longarm heard another door in the rear of the building open and shut. He managed a grin for Faye and said, "You got him so hot and bothered I reckon he had to take matters in hand."

She shivered in revulsion. "At least you'll get a decent meal before they haul you off to Mexico tomorrow." She passed the tray through the slot in the bars that had been made for that purpose.

Longarm looked at the food on the tray with anticipation. There were slices of roast beef in gravy, mashed potatoes, greens, and biscuits and honey. To one side were a deep-dish peach cobbler and a small jug of water. He looked up at Faye and smiled. "There's not really a gun in the mashed potatoes, is there?"

She shook her head. "I'm afraid not. And there's no Bowie knife in the cobbler." She leaned toward him and lowered her voice to a whisper. "*That's* where the gun is."

For a second, what she had said didn't penetrate Longarm's brain. Then he looked up at her again, more sharply this time. "What?"

"Just eat," she said. "You'll see when you get there. Don't take too long, though. There's no telling when Thurgood or one of the deputies will come back here."

Longarm knew that was right. In a normal tone of voice, just in case one of the deputies was eavesdropping, he said, "That peach cobbler looks so good, I think I'll have some of it first."

47

He dug in, and the cobbler *was* good. It took him only a moment to realize, however, that it wasn't quite as deep as it should have been, considering it was a deep-dish cobbler. Thurgood hadn't noticed that when he poked the fork into the pie. Obviously, the sheriff had thought the tines of the fork were scraping the bottom of the dish, rather than the thin piece of board Faye had evidently cut to fit perfectly inside the sloping walls of the vessel. That had left a hidden space about two inches deep at the bottom of the dish.

Longarm grinned. No two ways about it, Faye McCormick was a piece of work.

When he had the cobbler about half eaten, he was able to pry up the piece of board and lift out the little pistol Faye had hidden underneath it. The gun was a pocket revolver, the Remington Iroquois model. Only a .22-caliber, it wasn't much more than a kid's popgun, Longarm realized, but it would serve his purposes. At that, he was lucky to get it, since it was a little larger and heavier than most ladies' pocket pistols, and he assumed that it belonged to Faye. Moving quickly, he checked to see that it was fully loaded, then emptied the chamber under the hammer and put that cartridge in his shirt pocket. He tucked the gun away behind his belt at the small of his back, pulling out his shirttail a little to cover it. The piece of board, sticky with residue from the peach cobbler, went under the blanket on the cot. Longarm gave Faye a silent nod of thanks.

Then he went back to eating as if nothing had happened, putting the rest of the cobbler aside until he had finished the rest of the food. Then he polished off the remainder of the pie and washed it down with the last of the water from the jug. Longarm sighed. "Mighty good," he said, and meant it.

"Claude did the cooking," Faye said. "He's really sorry about what happened, Custis. He . . . he wanted to tell the truth, but he's afraid that if he tried to, the judge and the sheriff would shut down the cafe."

"You tell him it's all right," said Longarm. "I plan on doing something about Schofield and Thurgood once I serve out my sentence and go back to Denver."

"Is that so?" Thurgood's mocking voice came from the doorway, making Faye jump and give a little gasp of surprise.

Longarm had seen the sheriff lurking there, and his comment had been intended to bring a rise out of Thurgood as much as anything. He said, "That's right, Sheriff. You can't get away with treating a federal lawman—or any other law-abiding citizen—this way."

"Accordin' to all the evidence, you ain't a law-abidin' citizen, Long," Thurgood said. "You finished eatin'?"

"Yeah, I guess."

"Then give the tray to Miz McCormick and let her get on out of here. This ain't no place for a woman."

"I can't argue with that," said Longarm. He passed the tray back through the bars to Faye. "Much obliged, ma'am," he said to her. "You don't know how much that meal meant to me."

"I'm just glad I could help," Faye murmured.

"Come back any time," Thurgood told her with a leer as she left the cell block. He deliberately blocked part of the doorway so that she had to brush her body against his as she went by.

When Faye was gone, Thurgood ambled down the corridor to stand in front of Longarm's cell. "Hope you enjoyed that," he said. "You won't be gettin' food like that— or seein' a woman like her—for a long, long time."

"I reckon I can wait," Longarm said calmly.

"I reckon you ain't got much choice." Thurgood laughed. "But while you're down there in Mexico, don't you worry about Miz McCormick. I'm goin' to make it my special chore to sort of look out for her while you're gone, Long."

It would have been easy, so easy, right then to palm out that .22 and put a bullet right between the eyes of the crooked sheriff. Longarm took a deep breath and controlled the impulse. It would be better to wait.

Just not too long, he thought. Just not too long . . .

Chapter 6

This far south and west, in the middle of summer the sun didn't go down until late each day. Longarm wanted to wait until full darkness had fallen before he made his escape attempt, and the minutes seemed to creep by as he bided his time. Even after the sun had set, the garish red afterglow in the western sky provided too much light for Longarm's liking. He would have to sweat it out until the last of the sunlight faded.

As much as he would have liked to wreak his vengeance personally on Schofield, Thurgood, Clark, and the other deputies, he knew that wasn't practical. If he could get out of jail and get his hands on a horse, the thing to do would be to ride east as fast as he could toward the nearest railroad stop. There would be a telegraph office there, and he could send a wire to Billy Vail requesting some immediate aid to clear up the unholy mess in Inferno. Longarm figured the fact that Schofield was mixed up in some crooked alliance with a Mexican silver mine owner made this an international matter and therefore under the jurisdiction of the United States Justice Department. That was the tack he was going to take anyway, and if anybody didn't like it, they could take it up with him after Schofield and the others had gotten their comeuppance.

Finally, the shadows gathering around the town grew thick enough to cloak his movements once he was out of the jail, he decided. It was time to put his plan—such as it was—into action.

For the past hour, he had been listening carefully to the comings and goings of the other people in the building. The thick walls muffled the sounds somewhat, but by straining his ears, he was able to make a pretty good guess how many people were around. He thought everybody had left and gone home or out to supper except for a single deputy in the sheriff's office.

Longarm took the little pistol from behind his belt and checked it one more time, then let out a surprised-sounding yelp and called loudly, "Hey! Hey, out there in the office! I need some help in here!"

He heard a chair scrape back, followed by the heavy thud of booted feet on the floor. The only light in the cell block came from the barred window in the door, so when the deputy stuck his head up to the opening, he was silhouetted against the glow of the office lamp and Longarm couldn't make out his features. The man's voice was unfamiliar, though, as he asked, "What the hell do you want?"

"You better come in here," Longarm said ominously. "There's a snake in this cell, and I think it's a rattler."

"A rattler? How in blazes could a rattler get in there?"

"I don't know," replied Longarm, "but I heard it buzzing to beat the band just a minute ago, right under my bunk. Like to scared the shit out of me."

"Yeah, I heard that bleat you let out," said the deputy with a chuckle. "What do you want me to do about it?"

"Come in here and shoot the damned thing," Longarm said in exasperation. "I can't sleep with a snake crawling around." He paused, then added, "I don't reckon the judge would be too happy to lose a prisoner to a rattlesnake bite either."

"This is some sort of trick to get me in that cell so's you can jump me and get away," complained the deputy. "Hell, I'm smarter'n that."

52

Let's hope not, Longarm thought to himself. Aloud, he said, "You don't have to come into the cell. You can stand outside and shoot it. You'll be safe enough. *I'm* the one who's in danger of getting bit here."

"All right, all right, I reckon I can take a look." Longarm heard the rattle of keys at the door. "I suppose there might be a hole big enough somewhere in the back of the building for a snake to've crawled in."

While the guard was still fumbling with the keys, Longarm exclaimed, "Shit! There he goes rattling again!"

The deputy flung the door open and hurried into the cell block, already reaching for the six-gun holstered on his hip. "Where? I don't hear—"

He stopped short and stared at the barrel of the little pistol in Longarm's hand, which was looking him right in the eye.

The deputy had his hand on the butt of his revolver. Longarm was banking on the hope that the man didn't consider himself a shootist. If the deputy yanked his gun out and tried to throw down on Longarm, Longarm wouldn't have any choice but to go ahead and kill him—and hope that the body fell close enough to the cell so that Longarm could reach through the bars and get his hands on the keys. That was pretty unlikely.

Luck was with Longarm for just about the first time since he had ridden into Inferno, however. The deputy gulped, lifted his hand away from his gun, and said, "Don't shoot, mister. Lordy, please don't shoot."

"I won't unless you're a stupid son of a bitch," said Longarm. "Reach over real careful-like with your left hand, take that gun out, and put it on the floor. Don't drop it; bend over to set it down. I don't have to tell you not to yell, do I?"

The deputy's head moved back and forth in a rapid shake. "No, sir, you don't."

Now that Longarm had gotten a better look at the deputy, he could see the man was younger than the others he had encountered earlier in the day. He was tall and lanky and had a prominent Adam's apple. He wasn't one of the pair who had been with Clark during the fracas at Faye's house.

53

Likely he was the night man, Longarm decided, and not used to trouble.

"Sheriff Thurgood's goin' to *kill* me," moaned the deputy as he leaned over and placed his pistol on the floor as Longarm had ordered.

"Probably not," Longarm told him, "but I damned sure will unless you get over here and unlock this door right now."

"Mister, you're puttin' me in a hell of a spot."

"Not as bad as the one I'm in," Longarm said. "Now, move!"

The deputy swallowed hard a couple of times, then sighed and came over to the door of the cell, a ring of keys that he took from his belt in his hand. He unlocked the door and swung it open, then stepped back when Longarm motioned with the barrel of the little pistol.

"Where'd you get the gun?" asked the deputy. His face was pale in the light coming through the open cell block door.

"That's none of your business," Longarm said.

"I'll bet Mrs. McCormick brought it to you," the deputy went on. "Sheriff Thurgood ain't goin' to be happy about that."

The man was right, Longarm thought. Thurgood would blame Faye for this, and he had no doubt the sheriff would make her life miserable in retaliation. She might even be in danger.

Well, there was only one answer to this dilemma. When he left Inferno, he was just going to have to take Faye with him, whether she wanted to go or not. She could always return later, when Thurgood and Schofield and the others had been dealt with.

Longarm moved smoothly out of the cell into the corridor. The deputy looked disgustedly past him and said, "There wasn't really no snake in there, was there?"

Longarm shook his head. "Nope."

The deputy said a heartfelt "Shit." Then he looked at Longarm and asked, "Are you goin' to kill me?"

"Hadn't planned on it," Longarm answered honestly. He wanted to see this bunch of crooks behind bars, but not necessarily dead.

"Well, then, hit me on the head before you go," the deputy said bitterly. "It'll look a hell of a lot better to the sheriff if I've at least got a bump on my noggin when he finds out you're gone. Maybe he won't kill me."

Despite himself, Longarm felt a little liking for this man. Not much, because the deputy had undoubtedly participated in the scheme cooked up by Schofield and Thurgood . . . but a little. Longarm grinned and said, "Sure. Turn around." He had to make this quick, before Thurgood or one of the other deputies came back to the jail.

The deputy turned his back to Longarm, took his hat off, and screwed his eyes shut in seeming anticipation of the blow that was about to fall. Longarm stepped closer and lifted the hand holding the pistol.

Too late, he realized that the young deputy wasn't as guileless as he appeared to be. The man spun around suddenly and slashed out at Longarm with something he had taken from inside the sweatband of his hat. Longarm saw the flicker of polished steel and recognized the weapon the deputy held as a folding razor.

He had to jump back quickly to avoid getting his throat cut open. The deputy was a little off-balance, so Longarm stepped in and hooked a punch to the man's right side with his left hand. He didn't want to fire a shot unless he had to.

The blow knocked the deputy back even more, and his feet tangled with the three-legged stool on the far side of the corridor. He went over backwards with a yell.

Longarm leaped forward, hoping that shout hadn't been heard outside the jail. His arm rose and fell in a blur, and the butt of the pistol cracked against the deputy's skull. With a groan, the man went limp. He would be unconscious for a moment or two at least, Longarm knew.

Whirling around, Longarm scooped up the Colt .45 the deputy had placed on the floor. He tucked the smaller gun behind his belt again. The big Colt felt good in his hand. He hefted it as he hurried toward the cell block door.

He had just stepped into the sheriff's office when he heard the pounding of rapid footsteps approaching. Somebody passing by on the street outside could have heard the deputy's outcry and gone looking for the sheriff, Longarm thought fleetingly as he glanced around the room. He spotted another door in the wall opposite the main entrance and hoped it led to a rear exit. That would be his best bet.

He ran toward the other door, but just as he reached it, Thurgood, Clark, and another man burst in the front of the office. "There he is!" shouted Thurgood, and the gun that was already in his hand slammed a shot at Longarm. The bullet whipped past Longarm's ear and thudded into the rear wall of the office.

Longarm flung up the Colt in his hand and snapped a shot at Thurgood, but even as smoke and flame geysered from the barrel of the gun, he knew he had missed. Still, the shot served its purpose, because Thurgood and the two deputies ducked back into the hallway outside the office as the slug from Longarm's gun screamed past them. That gave Longarm the chance to reach the other door.

He grabbed the knob and twisted, realizing at that moment that he had no idea if the door was locked or not. There was no time for a sigh of relief as the knob turned under his hand. He yanked the door open and plunged through it as another bullet from Thurgood chewed splinters from the jamb only inches from his head.

Longarm found himself in a narrow corridor that led toward the back of the building. It probably ran alongside the cell block where he had spent the last few endless hours. As he sprinted toward the back door, he could hear yelling behind him and knew that Thurgood was probably sending somebody around to cover the rear of the building. There was no way they could get there before Longarm reached the door, though.

Luck was still with him. The door leading into the alley behind Inferno's single street was also unlocked. Longarm threw it open and ran out into the night. The air was still oppressively hot despite the darkness, but it smelled cleaner somehow outside the jail.

He turned to the left. The hotel was in that direction, he recalled, and Thurgood had said Longarm's horse was in the stable behind the hotel. If he wasn't able to reach the barn so that he could reclaim the dun, he would grab a horse off the street. The main thing was to get out of Inferno before Thurgood and the others caught up to him. Like it or not, he was going to have to leave Faye McCormick here for the time being and hope that Thurgood wouldn't hurt her.

Getting out of town was easier said than done, he realized a second later. Thurgood came running out the back door of the big stone building and triggered off another shot at him. Longarm heard the bullet whine past him, too damned close for comfort. He pivoted around to face Thurgood and went down to one knee, aiming to maybe shoot the sheriff's legs out from under him. The light back here was pretty weak for such fancy shooting, but that cut both ways.

Just as Longarm squeezed off his shot, however, Thurgood pitched to one side, sprawling face down on the ground. Around the corner of the building at that instant came the deputy Thurgood had sent around to cover the back door, arriving too late to do any good. Too late to do anything, in fact, except catch the slug Longarm had just fired right in his thigh. The deputy screamed and spun wildly to the ground, clutching his bullet-shattered leg.

Well, he had knocked down one of them, Longarm thought—just not the one he wanted.

If the deputy who owned the Colt was like most men, he kept only five rounds in the cylinder. That left Longarm three shots at the most. Longarm surged to his feet and started running again, as behind him Thurgood shouted furiously, ''Long, you bastard! I'll kill you!''

Thurgood tried to make good that boast by firing again, but once more the bullet whined off harmlessly into the night. Longarm reached an opening between two buildings and plunged into it, pounding toward the street. He was safe for the moment, out of the line of fire.

But not for long. He hadn't reached the street before a dark figure loomed up in front of him and fire lanced from the barrel of a revolver aimed at him.

Longarm heard the bullet whip past him as he instinctively sent a return shot at the muzzle flash of the other man's gun. The man staggered back and went to one knee. Longarm was close enough to him now to recognize him as one of the deputies who had jumped him at Faye's house. The man was trying to bring his pistol up again so that he could line the barrel on Longarm, but the gun seemed too heavy for him to lift. Longarm didn't hesitate when he reached the deputy.

He kicked the kneeling man square in the face.

The man went over backwards, out cold or at least out of the fight. Longarm vaulted over him and headed toward the hitch rack nearby where several saddled horses were tied. Longarm reached for the reins of the closest one, intending to jerk them loose and throw himself into the saddle.

A bullet struck the peeled pole hitch rack and threw splinters into the back of Longarm's hand. He jerked his arm away instinctively as Thurgood yelled from somewhere behind him, "There's the son of a bitch! Get him!"

At the same moment, Clark and another man dashed out from between two buildings farther up the street. They were in front of Longarm, Thurgood was behind him, and the bastards had him in a cross fire, he realized. He threw himself between two of the horses, using the bodies of the animals for cover. The horses were spooked by all the gunfire and yelling, though, and were already dancing around and jerking on their reins. If he didn't get stepped on, thought Longarm, it was only a matter of seconds until some of the horses broke free and bolted, and that would leave him out in the open again.

But if he swung up into one of the saddles, he would make himself a clear target for his pursuers. He was in deep trouble either way.

With enemies quickly closing in on him from both directions, Longarm leaned forward and yanked loose as many of the reins as he could reach. Then he grabbed a saddlehorn with his left hand and jammed his left foot into the saddle's right-side stirrup. He was taking a desperate chance, but if he could hang on to the side of the horse this way, he could still use the animals for cover as they stampeded down the street. He shouted, ''Yaaaahhh!'' then lifted his right leg and dangled there on the flank of the panicked horse as it whirled around and dashed down the street with the other horses.

The strain on his left arm and leg was tremendous, and his position was precarious to say the least. He wasn't even sure which direction the horses were going. But he might have gotten away if one of the other stampeding horses hadn't bumped heavily into him. The animal's shoulder thudded against Longarm and jolted his grip loose from the saddlehorn. He had no choice but to kick his foot free of the stirrup and let himself fall. Otherwise he would have been dragged to his death.

As it was, flying hooves almost crushed his skull, missing him only narrowly as he landed in the dusty street and rolled over several times. Somehow he had held on to the gun in his hand, and as he came up onto his knees, he looked around desperately for the nearest enemy.

The horse had carried him quite a distance down the street before he had fallen off, however, and while Thurgood and the deputies were running after him, for a second or two they would still be out of effective handgun range. Longarm lurched to his feet, seeing to his satisfaction that he was right in front of the hotel. He might still be able to reach the stable and get his hands on the dun.

But just as he started toward the hotel, the door of the building opened and Judge Hiram Schofield stepped out onto the plank boardwalk in front of the place. There was a double-barreled shotgun in the judge's hands, and the twin muzzles of the Greener started to lift quickly toward Longarm.

Biting back a curse because the way he wanted to go was blocked off to him, Longarm whirled and plunged into the thinning clouds of dust kicked up by the hooves of the stampeding horses. The dust would give him a little cover, but only for a few seconds.

He was going to have to have help to get out of town. He realized that now. Surely not everyone in Inferno was afraid of Schofield and Thurgood. If someone, anyone, would just lend him a hand . . .

That was when several men on horseback loomed up out of the night, trotting toward him. Longarm stopped in his tracks. There were half a dozen or more of them, and they appeared to be just riding into Inferno. They might not know what was going on here. Longarm couldn't see them very well because of the dust and the darkness, but he noted how straight they sat in their saddles and how their hats were all worn at the same angle. They looked like soldiers. By God, they *were* soldiers! Longarm thought.

And a troop of cavalry riding into Inferno would make all the difference in the world.

"Soldier blue!" he shouted as he ran toward them. "I'm a U.S. marshal! I need some help here!"

Then he came close enough to see that they weren't wearing cavalry uniforms at all. They were dressed in regular range clothes, although the garments were cleaner and better cared for than cowboy duds usually were. But they still sat their saddles like soldiers.

The man who was slightly in the lead reined in and said in a deep, vibrant voice, "Hold on there. A U.S. marshal, you say?"

"That's right!" Longarm began.

"Hey!" yelled Thurgood. "Step away from that man! He's an escaped prisoner!"

"That's a damned lie!" Longarm said. "I can prove who I am."

That was stretching the truth more than a little, but at least the arrival of these newcomers had caused the shooting to stop. Thurgood, Clark, and the other deputy faced the strangers somewhat nervously, while a short distance down the street, Judge Schofield still stood on the porch of the hotel, watching anxiously.

The man who seemed to be in charge of the strangers edged his horse forward a few more paces, and Longarm could see him better now in the light from the buildings along the street. He was tall and lean and carried himself with the dignified air of a man accustomed to being in charge. He looked at Longarm and said, "I think I believe you, sir."

Thurgood stepped forward and said angrily, "Just a damned minute! You can't come into my town—"

"It's not your town anymore," said the stranger. His hand came up with a gun in it. "It's mine."

Then he shot Thurgood in the chest.

Thurgood was rocked back by the shot, a mixture of shock and pain on his craggy face. He tried to lift his gun, but before he was able to do so, more shots came from the stranger, the slugs slamming into him and driving him backward in a macabre death dance. At the same time, some of the other men on horseback opened up on Clark and the other deputy as well, the hail of lead cutting them to bloody rags. Judge Schofield let out a curse of surprise and darted back into the hotel as fast as his considerable bulk would allow.

No one was more startled by all this than Longarm. He managed to yell, "What the hell!" before one of the strangers spurred forward and came up beside him. Longarm jerked his Colt up, but before he could fire the man had lashed out with the gun in his hand. The barrel cracked savagely against Longarm's skull and sent him spinning to the ground.

Longarm tasted dust and grit in his mouth and knew he had landed face-first in the street. But to him, it seemed as if he was still falling, plummeting through an empty blackness that grew darker and darker as he fell. He was utterly confused, and all he knew for certain was that Thurgood was dead, along with Clark and the other deputy. But he had no idea who the strangers were who had just gunned down Inferno's lawmen so unexpectedly.

He knew one other thing, Longarm remembered thinking, and that was that he had just been knocked out for the second time in less than twelve hours. He wondered if he would wake up from this one.

Then he didn't think anymore. He just kept falling, and falling, and falling. . . .

Chapter 7

This was getting to be a damned habit, Longarm thought as
he pushed himself upright and swung his legs off the cot in
the cell. When he had broken out of jail, his head had just
about stopped hurting from that first clout earlier in the day.
Now it was ringing like an anvil in Hades with Beelzebub
the blacksmith. He closed his eyes and held his head with
both hands, waiting for it to settle down.

For a moment, he had the crazy idea that none of the
events of the afternoon and evening had really happened.
Maybe he had just *imagined* waking up in the cell the first
time. That farce of a trial held by Judge Schofield, the meal
brought to him by Faye McCormick, the escape attempt that
had had such a bizarre ending . . . all of them could be fig-
ments of his dazed imagination. He heard a step on the other
side of the cell door and thought that when he opened his
eyes and looked up, he might well see Sheriff Carl Thurgood standing there, ready to torment him some more, rather
than lying out in the street shot to pieces.

Instead, a hard-faced young man in neat range clothes
stood in the cell block corridor, his clean-cut features show-
ing a little curiosity but not much as he gazed at Longarm.

"Do you require medical attention, sir?" asked the young
man.

Longarm blinked and was silent for a long moment before he replied, "Only if you can find one of those newfangled doctors from Europe that treat fellas who are addled in the head."

He saw a faint hint of a smile on the young man's lips. "Our medical officer is quite skilled at patching up bullet wounds, but I doubt that he has the requisite skills to deal with such a problem as you describe."

"Just a regular army sawbones, eh?"

"You might say so."

"I might say a lot of things . . . like who the hell are you and what in blazes is going on around here?"

This time the young man did smile, although it was a small one. "I'm afraid I'm not authorized to give you that information."

Wearily, Longarm massaged his temples and then scrubbed his hand over his face. Maybe if he would just lie down again on the cot, turn his face to the wall, and sleep for a while, all this would be gone when he woke up, he thought.

But he knew that wouldn't be the case. He wasn't crazy, he wasn't dreaming, he wasn't seeing things from being clouted on the head twice in one day. Whatever was happening in Inferno tonight, it was *real*.

The sound of more footsteps made Longarm look toward the door between the cell block and the sheriff's office. An older man who was somewhat stocky and sported a neatly trimmed dark beard stood there dressed in whipcord trousers, a white shirt, and a black vest. A black Stetson was on his head. He carried himself with the same military bearing as the young man just outside the cell.

"Is the prisoner awake again, Lieutenant Carson?" asked the bearded man.

"Yes, sir," replied the younger man. "Orders, Major?"

"Continue watching him," grunted the major. "The colonel's not finished with the other one yet, but I'm sure he'll want to talk to this prisoner too."

Lieutenant, thought Longarm. *Major and colonel.* These gents were definitely military, despite their civilian clothes.

Or ex-military anyway. He couldn't imagine any real soldiers riding into a town and shooting down the local star-packers with no warning unless they had completely turned renegade.

Longarm had heard of other army outfits that had deserted en masse and turned to outlawry. It could be that he had just run across one of them.

The bearded major went back into the sheriff's office, while Lieutenant Carson continued to stand stiffly just outside the cell. Longarm gave the young man a humorless grin and said, "At ease, son. You'll make your backbone sore standing at attention like that. Just how long do you reckon I'll be locked up in here anyway?"

"I really couldn't say, sir," Carson replied.

Longarm leaned back against the stone wall behind him. More to make conversation and pass the time than anything else, he said, "Were you part of the bunch that rode into town while I was trying to get away from Thurgood and his men?"

"I accompanied the colonel on his initial foray into the settlement, yes."

"Then you must have noticed how those fellas were trying to shoot me."

"Of course."

"Didn't you wonder what it was about?"

There was genuine bafflement on Carson's face as he said, "We had our orders, sir. There were no other considerations."

Longarm heaved a sigh. If they were all like Carson, they were a well-disciplined bunch. That was another bit of evidence pointing to their army background.

Figuring that he wasn't going to get much more information from the young man, Longarm was content to sit there in silence for a while and nurse his aching head. He had already decided that he didn't want to make too much of a fuss about being a federal lawman. If these men were ex-army renegades, he couldn't represent anything to them except a threat. No need to remind them of how he had identified himself as a United States marshal right after they rode into town.

Besides, he had a feeling that the colonel Carson had mentioned hadn't forgotten about it.

A few minutes later, the door into the cell block opened again, and a thickset figure came stumbling through it. Judge Hiram Schofield caught his balance by grabbing hold of the cell bars. When he looked up, his eyes met Longarm's.

Under other circumstances, Longarm might have enjoyed seeing Schofield taken down a notch or two. The judge's clothes were disheveled, his thinning hair was askew, and there were bruises on his face. Obviously, he had put up a fight when the men who had invaded Inferno captured him. Equally obviously, struggling hadn't done him any good. He was just as much a prisoner now as Longarm was.

The bearded major came into the cell block right behind Schofield. He nodded to Carson and said, "Open the door, Lieutenant. This one is going in the cell too."

Schofield looked wildly over his shoulder at the major. "Not in there!" he exclaimed. "Don't put me in with that man!"

Longarm came to his feet and took a step toward the bars. "What's the matter, Judge?" he asked dryly. "Don't like the idea of being locked up with the same man you sentenced earlier today?"

Schofield looked at Longarm again, his eyes wide. The major stepped forward and said sharply, "Here now, there'll be none of that. Lieutenant Carson, I'm counting on you to maintain order in here once both prisoners have been locked up."

"Yes, sir, of course," Carson said briskly as he put his hand on the butt of his holstered revolver. "The colonel's not ready for this one yet?"

"Not quite. He'll send word when he wants the other prisoner brought to him. For now, just lock up this one."

"Yes, sir." Carson took the ring of keys and unlocked the cell door, then swung it wide and stepped back. "Get inside, mister."

With an obvious effort, Schofield drew himself up and tried to recapture some of his lost dignity. He hooked his thumbs in his rumpled vest and said, "That's 'Judge.' Judge Hiram Schofield, young man. You and the rest of your gang will regret treating me like this."

The major prodded Schofield in the back. "Just get inside and save the speeches for later."

Schofield shuffled into the cell, still casting nervous glances in Longarm's direction. Longarm backed off a little. He certainly hadn't forgotten the justifiable grudge he held against Schofield, but it appeared that they now shared a common enemy . . . a dangerous enemy. Longarm was a little surprised he and Schofield hadn't been gunned down like Thurgood and the deputies.

The colonel had a reason for keeping them alive. Longarm was sure of that. He hadn't met the colonel except for that brief encounter in the street, but he was certain the man never did *anything* without having a reason for his actions.

Carson shut the cell door with a clang and relocked it. Schofield moved toward the cot, warily watching Longarm from the corner of his eye as he did so. Longarm stayed where he was. At the moment, he wanted information more than he wanted revenge on Schofield.

The judge straightened his coat and sat down, being careful not to look at Longarm now. The major appeared satisfied, because he nodded and turned to leave the cell block. Carson stopped him by saying, "Major Niland?"

The major turned back. "What is it, Lieutenant?"

"How much latitude do I have in maintaining order?"

Niland considered, then said, "Don't kill either of them. But they don't have to be able to walk. You can shoot them in the knee if you have to."

"Yes, sir. Thank you, sir."

Longarm didn't much care for the easy way Carson accepted that suggestion.

"I don't plan to cause any trouble," he said to the lieutenant as Niland went back into the sheriff's office.

"Don't believe him, Lieutenant," said Schofield. "This man caused nothing but havoc in my town after he rode in this morning. He's a born troublemaker.''

Longarm chuckled grimly. ''Sounds like you've grown some balls in the last few minutes, Your Honor. Wasn't it you who was afraid to be put in here with me?''

''That's enough,'' snapped Carson. ''I don't want the two of you harassing each other. Major Niland won't like it if I have to break up a fight, but I'll do whatever is necessary to maintain order. You can believe that.''

Carson reminded Longarm of some of the young officers he had served under during the Late Unpleasantness: stiff-necked, devoted to their duty, and not overly bright. ''Don't worry, Lieutenant,'' Longarm said to him. ''The judge and me, we're past whatever trouble was between us—at least for the time being.''

''You'll forgive me if I fail to completely believe that noble sentiment,'' Schofield said in a frosty voice.

Longarm shrugged. ''Suit yourself.'' He put his back against one of the stone walls of the cell and slid down it to sit cross-legged on the floor.

Carson seemed to relax a little after a few minutes went by. Longarm ignored the young officer and asked in a quiet voice, ''What happened out there after I was knocked out, Schofield?''

The judge seemed reluctant to answer for a moment, but finally, after a nervous glance in Carson's direction, he said, ''More of them rode in. That first bunch was just the advance party. Once they heard the shooting, they swept in and took over the whole town. Must've been twenty or thirty of them.''

Longarm nodded. Carson's face was carefully expressionless in the light from a lantern hung on a peg on the wall just inside the cell block door. But Longarm could tell that the young man was listening.

Thinking about Faye, Longarm asked, ''Was there a lot of killing?''

Schofield shook his head. ''I don't think anyone was killed except Sheriff Thurgood and his deputies. There wasn't a shot fired after that.'' The judge cleared his throat as if he was embarrassed. "The odds were simply too over-whelming."

Longarm considered that statement. He estimated there were over a hundred people in Inferno, and Schofield had already said the invading force contained fewer than forty men. Those odds didn't sound too overwhelming to him.

But the citizens had grown accustomed to allowing Scho-field, Thurgood, and their cronies to run things around here. It had taken a much smaller force than forty men to com-pletely cow the people of this community. Longarm's mouth tightened into a grim line. No wonder the colonel and his men had been able to waltz in and take over so easily.

"Do you know what happened to Mrs. McCormick?"

Schofield shook his head. "I have no idea. I haven't seen the lady all evening."

"What happened after they nabbed you?" asked Long-arm.

"I was taken over to the hotel to see . . . to see their com-mander. The one they call the colonel."

The tall, lean man who had been leading the advance party, thought Longarm. He had no doubt that was the colo-nel. The man had carried himself with such an air of su-periority and command that he could not have been anyone else.

"He . . . he asked if I was in charge here in Inferno, and I admitted that I was," Schofield went on. "He assured me that no one else would be harmed if we all just cooperated with him and his men."

"And I reckon you promised him you sure would," Longarm said dryly.

Schofield folded his arms across his chest and scowled. "I have a responsibility to the citizens. I have to do what I think is best for them."

"Especially when it keeps you from getting killed like Thurgood."

Schofield just glowered at him and didn't say anything.

After a moment, Longarm went on. "What else did the colonel say to you?"

"He asked me about the train schedule," Schofield replied, and his frown turned to one of genuine puzzlement. "I told him the next train through here would be the westbound tomorrow morning. It always stops to take on water around dawn."

Longarm thought about that, then said, "I'll bet he was glad to hear that, wasn't he?"

"He seemed to be," Schofield confirmed.

Longarm leaned his head back against the stone wall and closed his eyes. There was still a pounding ache behind his forehead, and even worse than that was the feeling that he didn't know what the hell was going on. He had a glimmering of an idea, but he needed a lot more information before he decided what to do about it.

As if he could do anything while he was locked up in jail like this, he thought bitterly. He was trapped good and proper, and it wouldn't be as easy to escape from these captors. Thurgood and the deputies had been arrogant and lazy, too accustomed to having everything go their way with little or no resistance.

The colonel and his men were vastly different and even more dangerous. Longarm had to be absolutely sure of what he was doing before he made his move.

But sooner or later he would have to do *something*. He couldn't let the capture of an entire town go unchallenged. He might be the only one in Inferno willing to stand up to the invaders, but if that was the case, then so be it.

And if all he managed to do was get himself killed, that was all right too. At least he would go down fighting.

For now, however, he was content to wait. Sooner or later, he would be face-to-face with the colonel.

Maybe then he would find out what this was all about.

Chapter 8

A few more minutes passed while Longarm brooded in silence. Schofield wasn't feeling very talkative either. Maybe his conscience was gnawing on him, Longarm mused. If that was the case, it was damned well about time. There was nothing like peering into the face of death to make a man take stock of himself.

The cell block door opened again, and Major Niland strode into the corridor. Gesturing toward Longarm, he said, "The colonel's ready for that one now. Bring him out."

"Yes, sir," said Lieutenant Carson. The young man unlocked the door as Longarm climbed slowly to his feet. Carson stepped back and slid his gun from leather to cover Longarm.

Longarm glanced at Schofield, who was still sitting on the cot with his head down in a pose of despair. With a grimace, Longarm turned away from the judge and stepped out into the corridor. Niland had drawn his gun as well, and both he and Carson covered Longarm as the deputy marshal walked out into the sheriff's office. Carson slammed the cell door on the way.

There was an escort waiting there for him, he found. Four men with Winchesters in their hands stood inside the office. Like Niland and Carson, they were dressed in new-looking range garb. Despite the differences in their outfits, the

71

clothes still looked like uniforms to Longarm. The military atmosphere was that strong.

"We'll take the prisoner down the street to the hotel," Niland said to the four men. "Watch him closely. The colonel says he's a dangerous man."

Longarm smiled thinly. "Reckon I'll have to thank this colonel of yours for the compliment."

"Just answer his questions and I'm sure you'll get along fine," Niland snapped. "Let's go."

The little group left the sheriff's office and went down the main hallway outside to the front door of the big stone building. Two of the guards flanked Longarm, while the other two men and Niland brought up the rear. Longarm had no doubt the major's gun was aimed right at his back. Niland might be under orders not to kill him, but a hell of a lot of damage could be done without being fatal. Longarm wasn't going to tempt fate.

Not just yet anyway.

The street was empty of citizens when they went outside, Longarm saw. Members of the renegade troop were stationed along the way, standing guard as Longarm would have expected. Obviously, all the civilians were lying low. Longarm wondered if the sentries had orders to shoot on sight anybody they saw moving around the town. He wouldn't put it past the colonel.

The hotel was the second-largest building in Inferno. It was a two-story frame structure, and the lumber to build it had probably been freighted in from up around Flagstaff, Longarm thought as he and the other men approached it. He was marched into the lobby, where he saw his first citizen in a while, other than Schofield. A scared-looking room clerk with slicked-down hair parted in the middle stood behind the desk. Something about that struck Longarm as incongruous. It was pretty damned unlikely anybody else was going to be arriving tonight.

More folks might leave, so to speak, before morning came, though.

"Upstairs," Niland grunted. "And when we get there, keep a civil tongue in your head. The colonel won't tolerate any disrespect."

"I'll keep that in mind," Longarm said. He didn't try very hard to keep the sarcasm out of his voice.

He climbed the stairs next to the desk, feeling the eyes of the rabbity clerk on him as he did so. Longarm wondered if the gent was looking to him for some sort of miraculous salvation. Longarm intended to do the best he could, but it would be a lot easier if the people of Inferno would just wake up and get a little steel in their backbones.

"Down the hall," Niland ordered when they reached the top of the stairs. "We're going to Room Nine."

That was at the front of the hotel, overlooking Inferno's only real street, Longarm judged. And not surprisingly, it was also the best room in the house, he saw as the two men already on guard beside the door opened it and ushered him inside. The escort that had brought him here stayed outside, with the exception of Major Niland. The major followed Longarm into the room and said, "Here he is, Colonel, just like you ordered."

The tall man stood at one of the pair of windows overlooking the street. The curtain was pulled back so that he could peer out at the night through the glass. He turned and gave Niland a curt nod. "Thank you, Major," he said in his deep, mellifluous voice. "You're dismissed."

Niland frowned. "Colonel, are you sure it's a good idea to leave the two of you—"

"I said that you are dismissed, Major," the colonel repeated. "I take it you remember the meaning of that command?"

His back stiffening, Niland replied, "Yes, sir. My apologies, sir."

The colonel waved a hand. "That's all right, Major. I understand your concern. But I don't think you need to worry about Marshal Long. He'll cause no trouble."

"Yes, sir. I'll be outside if you need me." Niland backed out of the door and closed it behind him.

Coolly, Longarm regarded the colonel. "You're mighty confident I won't start a ruckus," he commented. "I ain't feeling very kindly toward you and your pards right about now."

The colonel chuckled. "No, I imagine not. But I know you won't try anything yet, Marshal, because your curiosity hasn't been satisfied. You want to know what this is all about, don't you?"

Longarm inclined his head in acknowledgment of the other man's point.

The colonel reached into the pocket of his vest and brought out a couple of cigars. "Smoke?" he asked, extending one of the cheroots toward Longarm.

The gesture threw Longarm a bit, but only for a second. He said, "Sure," and reached out to take the cigar from the colonel.

He was close enough now that he could have jumped the man, might have even been able to get his hand on the butt of the revolver the colonel wore holstered on his right hip. But that would have just brought the guards rushing in from the corridor outside; and besides, the colonel had him pegged: He wanted to know what was going on here. Longarm had a feeling the colonel was going to tell him, at least part of it.

The colonel scratched a lucifer into life and lit both their smokes, then shook the match out. As Longarm took a deep, satisfying drag on the cheroot, he studied the man who was in charge of the force that had taken over Inferno.

Longarm and the colonel were about the same height and had the same sort of rangy, powerful build. They shared as well the deep tan of men who spent their time outdoors. The colonel wore pin-striped trousers tucked into high-topped black boots and a dark gray coat over a black vest and white shirt. The only real touch of color about him was the red bandanna tied around his neck. Longarm recalled that General Custer had favored a red bandanna like that. In Longarm's opinion it just made a fella a better target when somebody was shooting at him.

A flat-crowned gray hat had been set aside, revealing short, graying brown hair on the colonel's head. He was clean-shaven. His features were too craggy to be called handsome, but Longarm suspected he was attractive to women. There was a vitality about him that would draw just about anybody to him.

As long as you didn't look too closely at his eyes. Then you'd see the cold deadness there and know that the best thing to do would be to turn around and run in the opposite direction.

Longarm didn't feel much like running. He took the cheroot from his mouth, blew smoke toward the ceiling, and said, "I reckon introductions are in order. I'm—"

"Custis Long," the colonel said. "Yes, Marshal, I know your name. Judge Schofield told me. I'm not sure he believed you about being a federal lawman, however."

"Schofield didn't care who I was," said Longarm. "To him I was just one more unlucky son of a bitch who fell into the trap he and Sheriff Thurgood had set."

"So I gathered. But for what it's worth, Marshal Long, I *do* believe you. I've heard of you more than once. You're the famous Longarm, deputy to Chief Marshal Billy Vail in Denver."

Stifling a groan, Longarm said, "I surely do wish those reporters would quit writing such fancy stories about me in the Denver papers."

"Oh, it's not just in Denver," said the colonel. "Your name has popped up in connection with cases from El Paso to the Canadian border, sometimes beyond. The Mexicans call you Brazo Largo."

"Them that don't call me other, less polite names."

The colonel smiled. "Well, I, for one, am pleased to meet you, Marshal. My name is Thaddeus Vickery."

"Colonel Thaddeus Vickery?" The name didn't mean anything to Longarm.

"Ex-colonel, actually. But I encourage the use of our former ranks among my men. It enables us to maintain the discipline necessary to carry out our missions."

"Then you're not really in the army anymore," Longarm said.

Vickery's lips tightened on the cigar in his mouth. "Some men never truly leave the army—it leaves them."

"You and your men got drummed out?" Longarm knew he was taking a chance by asking such a blunt question; he wouldn't have given a nickel for Vickery's mental stability. But he still wanted to know exactly what—and who—he was dealing with here.

"My men and I are patriots, Marshal. That's all you need to know." Vickery's tense stance relaxed slightly. "I'd offer you a drink, but I'm afraid I don't allow my men to use alcohol during a mission."

"I'm not under your command, Colonel," Longarm pointed out—rather unnecessarily, he thought.

"No, but I still try to discourage drinking except under certain circumstances. When we return to our headquarters, then the men will be allowed to indulge."

Might as well try for some more answers, decided Longarm. "And where might those headquarters be?"

Vickery smiled and said, "That's another of those things you don't really need to know, Marshal Long." He puffed on his cigar, then asked, "What brings you to Inferno? I'm at a loss to understand how you could have heard of our mission—unless we have a traitor in the ranks, which I think is highly unlikely."

"Pure dumb luck," replied Longarm. "I was chasing a prisoner. He made it over the border ahead of me, so I had to turn around and start home. This was the first place I came to where I could get some grub and a bed for a few hours." He shook his head. "The stopover didn't work out too well."

"Perhaps it won't go too badly for you. You've been saved from whatever dismal fate Judge Schofield had in store for you, and as long as you cooperate, there's a very good chance you'll still be alive when we leave here."

"After you've met that westbound train first thing in the morning, you mean?"

Vickery's eyes narrowed in suspicion. Clearly, he hadn't expected Longarm to know anything about the true purpose of the invasion of Inferno. After a moment he shrugged. "I suppose the judge must have told you that I inquired about

76

the train schedule, and you inferred that that is why we're here.''

"I've been a lawman for a pretty good spell," said Longarm. "I know how an owlhoot's mind works most of the time.''

Vickery snorted in derision. "We are *not* owlhoots, as you put it, Marshal. We have a mission here, and we intend to carry it out successfully. We will indeed be meeting that train in the morning when it stops to take on water. But when our business is concluded, we'll be leaving Inferno, and no one else will be harmed as long as everyone in town does as they're told.''

"Why did you shoot the sheriff and his men?"

"A precaution," answered the colonel. "We've found that when the local authorities are eliminated immediately, the citizens are much more likely to cooperate. You and Judge Schofield were spared, however, because I have something more important in mind for the two of you.''

"You want us around in case something goes wrong and you need hostages," Longarm guessed.

Vickery grimaced. "Unfortunately, you are correct, Marshal. I despise the very idea of using hostages. That means the plan has failed somehow, and I'm vain enough to think that my plans should never fail. It's very difficult to take everything into consideration, though. Life can be so . . . strange sometimes.''

"That's the damned truth," Longarm said under his breath.

Vickery set what was left of his cigar in an ashtray on the room's table, then faced Longarm and clasped his hands behind his back. "Are you sure, Marshal Long, that your presence here in Inferno is nothing but an accident?''

"I sure as hell didn't come here on purpose," Longarm declared. "And if I could ride out right now and never hear of the place again, I'd do it.''

"Oh, I doubt that. Your sense of duty is too strong to abandon a town in trouble. Not to mention that the mystery of the whole affair would drive you insane if it was left unsolved. I know that because you and I are much alike,

Marshal. I could never turn my back on my duty either.''

Heading up a pack of murderous gunmen didn't sound like any sort of duty Longarm had ever heard of, but he kept the thought to himself. He didn't want to push Vickery too far just yet.

"So," Vickery said after a moment, "I'm left with something of a dilemma. I believe that you are an honorable man, Marshal Long, so I think you're telling me the truth when you say that you have no real knowledge of our plans. At the same time, you represent a very real danger. Judge Schofield is not an overly brave man, but he would make a fine hostage. You might not. The intelligent thing to do with you would be to kill you right here and now.''

If Vickery reached for his gun, Longarm thought, he would jump the colonel and try to bust out through one of those windows before the guards rushed in from the corridor. He would rather take a chance on busting an arm or a leg—or his head—than just stand there and let himself be gunned down. Before he went out the window, though, he would do his dead-level best to kill this crazy bastard who called himself a colonel. Longarm made that promise to himself.

Vickery made no move toward his pistol, however. He simply regarded Longarm with an unreadable expression for a long moment, then nodded. "I'm going to keep you alive," he said. "You're the first man I've met in a long time who I sense could give me an actual challenge. Not that you'll ever have the chance, mind you, Longarm. You don't mind if I call you Longarm, do you?''

"Call me anything you want, old son.''

Vickery strolled toward the door, circling wide around Longarm so that he stayed outside of arm's reach. He said, "I want to prove to you that I'm not a complete monster, Marshal. I have something you want, and I'm willing to give it to you.''

Longarm couldn't think of anything Vickery might have that he would want, and he was about to say so when it hit him what the colonel was talking about. The knowledge was like a cold fist in the middle of his gut.

Vickery opened the door and said, "Bring the lady in, Major."

Longarm heard Niland's voice replying crisply, "Yes, sir."

Vickery turned back to him and went on. "Judge Schofield is a very talkative man. He told me everything I wanted to know about Inferno and its inhabitants. For example, he explained that you seemed to have already made a good friend here despite your short stay in this settlement."

Major Niland appeared in the doorway, pushing a very frightened-looking Faye McCormick in front of him. Longarm hadn't seen her since she had brought his supper to the jail. That seemed like days ago, rather than mere hours. Faye was wearing the same dress, and she was lovely despite the fear that drew her features into a taut mask.

"Hello, Mrs. McCormick," Vickery said smoothly. "I believe you know everyone here."

Suddenly, Faye tore her arm out of Niland's grip and ran across the room to Longarm, throwing herself into his arms. He tightened them around her protectively as she buried her face against his broad chest. "It's all right, darlin'," he said quietly. "It's all right now."

"It certainly is," said Vickery, "and it will remain so as long as you understand one thing quite clearly, Marshal Long." His voice hardened. "Cooperate with us, do as you're told, and no one will harm Mrs. McCormick. But if you don't . . . I'll kill her, Marshal. I won't hesitate to blow her brains out."

Chapter 9

"All right," Longarm said after a moment of tense silence. "You've got a deal, Vickery. Leave Mrs. McCormick alone, and I'll do anything you say."

At that instant, Longarm didn't know if he was lying or not. He had grown very fond of Faye in a short time, and he had no doubt Vickery meant every word of the threat he had made.

But the colonel was a cold-blooded murderer. It would go against every instinct that was ingrained in Longarm's body to allow such a killer to go about his work unhindered. Somebody had to put a stop to whatever monstrous scheme Vickery had hatched, and there was no one else in Inferno to do that except Longarm.

He put the moral dilemma aside for the time being and concentrated on reassuring the sobbing woman in his arms. "I won't let 'em hurt you, Faye," he told her in a quiet voice.

"Very touching," Vickery said, a hint of mockery in his tone. "Remember, Longarm, her fate—and yours—will be in your hands." He picked up the still-smoldering butt of his cigar and put it back in his mouth. Around the cheroot, he went on. "Now, to prove to you that I'm not a complete villain, I'm going to give the two of you some privacy. I have matters of my own to attend to." He reached out and picked up his flat-crowned gray hat. "I'm going to leave the two of you here together. Feel free to make any use of the room that you please. But be aware of the fact that there will be armed men right outside the door, as well as on the porch of the hotel and the roof. If either of you tries to escape through the door or the windows, you'll be shot down without hesitation. While I'd prefer to keep both of you alive, it's not an absolute necessity."

"I understand," Longarm said grimly.

Vickery settled the hat on his head. "I thought you would," he said.

He went to the door, gave them a deceptively cordial nod, then stepped out into the corridor. As the door shut, Longarm heard the colonel issuing low-voiced orders to the men who stood guard just outside.

Longarm still had Faye in his embrace. He felt her draw a deep, shuddery breath; then she tilted her head back so that she could look up at him. Quietly, calmly, she said, "I thought that son of a bitch would never leave."

A little surprised by her demeanor, Longarm looked down at her and studied her lovely features. It was true that her cheeks were streaked with the trails of the tears she had shed, but her eyes were clear now. Sure, there was still some fear in her expression, but that nearly panic-stricken terror she had exhibited earlier had utterly vanished.

Longarm chuckled. "You're a hell of an actress, Faye," he said, keeping his voice pitched low so that it wouldn't carry to Vickery's men in the hallway outside the room. "You weren't near as scared as you were putting on, were you?"

"Oh, I was scared, all right," she admitted. "I still am. But I'm mad too. Who does that Colonel Vickery think he is? He can't just come in and take over a whole town and start shooting people!"

Longarm took a step back and put his hands on Faye's shoulders. "That's exactly what he did, and so far, he's gotten away with it."

"Well, somebody's got to stop him," she said stubbornly.

Longarm frowned. Faye seemed almost like a different woman from the one who had tried to get him not to start any trouble when Davey was harassing him in the cafe that morning. She had been as much under the thumb of Schofield, Thurgood, the deputies, and Schofield's ranch hands as everybody else in Inferno. Now, though, she had been changed, transformed somehow.

"What happened to you, Faye? Did Vickery's men hurt you?"

She shook her head. "No, I . . . I just got tired of all of it. Tired of just giving in and letting other people run roughshod over me because it was the easiest thing to do. Judge Schofield and his bunch were bad enough, but this crazy colonel is the last straw."

Everybody had a breaking point, thought Longarm, a point at which they would turn and fight, no matter what the odds against them. Faye McCormick had reached hers tonight.

He wished the same thing held true of some of the other good citizens of Inferno.

"Vickery's not really a colonel," he told her. "Maybe he was once, I don't know, but now he's just an outlaw who fancies himself some sort of military leader. I think he and his bunch plan to rob the westbound train when it comes in at dawn tomorrow morning."

"So to do that he takes over a whole town?"

It seemed like an unnecessarily drastic plan to Longarm too, but there was no telling what went on in the mind of a man like Vickery. Longarm shrugged, then said, "Schofield told me nobody has been killed since Thurgood and his men were gunned down. Is that true?"

"I think so. Vickery's men spread out over the town and herded everybody into the street at gunpoint. Then he made a speech to us about how nobody else would be hurt if we followed orders. We were told to go back to our houses and businesses and stay inside for the rest of the night. Then he posted guards all up and down the street to enforce his orders."

Longarm nodded. "Reckon I was still out cold while all this was going on."

Faye lifted a hand to his head and touched it tenderly. "Are you all right, Custis?" she asked. "You've gotten knocked out twice today."

"You're not telling me anything I don't already know," he said with a chuckle. "But I'm not seeing double or anything, and the headache I had when I woke up earlier is starting to ease up now. No ringing in my ears either, nor any dizziness. I reckon this old skull of mine is so thick that nothing can hurt it . . . short of maybe getting kicked by a mule."

"Well, you're lucky. I want you to be careful. You don't need to get hit in the head again."

"I'll try to remember that," Longarm said dryly.

She grinned at him in a mixture of exasperation and affection, then grew more serious and asked, "What are we going to do now?"

"I'm not sure yet," replied Longarm with a shake of his head. "You heard Vickery. If I try anything, it'll be risking your life."

"You can't worry about that," she said, her voice still quiet but taking on a tone of fierceness now. "Vickery's plan has to be stopped, and we're the only ones who can do it."

"Maybe so, but if you wound up getting hurt—"

She stopped him by grabbing his arms, coming up on her toes, and pressing her mouth hard against his in a kiss that mixed passion and desperation. Longarm was startled by her action, but he grasped her arms and pulled her against him as he returned the kiss. Faye's mouth opened, inviting his tongue inside with an urgent appeal that could not be denied. Longarm probed the hot, wet cavern of her mouth. Her tongue returned the caress, flicking and circling around his.

When they finally broke the kiss, Longarm began, "Well, that was a mite surprising—"

"Make love to me, Custis," she interrupted. "Make love to me now."

Longarm frowned and cast a glance at the door of the room. "Vickery's guards are right outside," he reminded her.

"I don't care!" she hissed. "I need you, Custis Long. We don't know what's going to happen between now and tomorrow, but right now, I need you to hold me. I need to feel you inside me." She pressed her cheek against his chest. "I'm sorry to be so bold," she whispered. "There's just not enough time to be any other way."

"It's all right," he murmured, stroking her hair. "I reckon I understand. I want you too."

His hand slid down her back to the curve of her hips. Gently, he kneaded the smooth swell of her backside. She slipped both arms around his waist and clung tightly to him as he moved his other hand to her bottom, cupped both cheeks, and pressed her stomach against his groin. His erect shaft prodded the softness of her belly through their clothes.

Longarm began working the back of her dress up, bunching the material around her waist. His hands slid inside her panties and found warm, silky flesh. He trailed a fingertip down the cleft of her buttocks, sending a shiver of delight through her. With his other hand, he reached around and found the folds of her femininity. His fingers delved into the wet heat of her core, prompting her hips to jerk against him.

There was no time for this, no way of knowing when Vickery might return. But the need was too great in both of them to be put aside. What Faye had said was true: There was no telling what the future might bring. So they had to take full advantage of the present. *Carpe diem*, as those old-timers who talked Latin would say, Longarm thought. Holding tightly to Faye's hips, he picked her up and carried her toward the bed.

They didn't waste a lot of time removing clothes. They just lifted some things and shoved aside others, and suddenly Longarm's shaft was in Faye's hands and she was lying on her back with her legs spread wide open. Faye held his massive pole with both hands for a moment, using her thumb to spread the pearl of moisture that had already seeped from the head of the shaft. Then she brought it to her honeyed opening and stared into his eyes, her mouth open a little, as a surge of his hips sheathed him inside her, filling her.

"Oh, Custis!" she gasped.

Immediately, he launched into a pounding, pulsating rhythm that brought his shaft nearly out of her before it plunged back in on each downstroke. It was pure and elemental and had both of them clutching at each other and breathing hard in a matter of seconds. Longarm drove in and out of her as their passion built and built and finally crested. His climax erupted out of him in thick, scalding jets, and at the same instant Faye mashed her mouth against his to stifle the scream of ecstasy that tried to well up her throat. Longarm felt her muscles spasming intimately around him, the buttery walls milking every last drop of juice from him with an incredibly tender strength.

Sated, Longarm loomed over her for a moment, supporting his weight with his hands planted on the bed on either side of her head; then he rolled to the side and flopped onto his back to draw in several deep breaths. Faye found his hand and took hold of it with both of hers. She brought it to her lips and kissed the back of it. Longarm looked over at her.

"You and I, we've had more in twelve hours than some folks find in a lifetime, Custis," she whispered. "Now, you've got to promise me you won't let Vickery get away with whatever he's planning, no matter what."

Longarm lifted himself on an elbow to peer down at her. "That's not the only reason you—"

She stopped him with a finger on his lips. "Of course not," she said. She traced her finger along the lines of his mustache. "But I still want you to promise me."

Longarm sighed. He knew as well as she did that Vickery's plan had to be stopped. He nodded.

With a smile, Faye said, "Come on, we'd better get ourselves straightened up again." She swung her legs off the bed and stood up, turning her back toward Longarm as she made some mysterious female adjustments to her clothes.

For his part, he got to his feet and buttoned up, then brushed the cover on the bed smooth again. Their lovemaking had been intense but fairly quiet. It was possible not even the guards outside the room knew what had really happened.

"All right," said Faye when she faced him again, "what are we going to do? Do we jump Vickery when he comes back up here?"

"I'm not sure that would do much good," Longarm said as he rasped a thumbnail along the line of his jaw in thought. "He's got too many men close by. What we need to do is get him off by himself somewhere."

"How can we do that?" asked Faye.

"Let me think on it."

Unfortunately, there was no time to think. Brisk footsteps sounded just outside the door, and it swung open again a moment later. Vickery came into the room.

By that time, Longarm and Faye were on opposite sides of the room. Vickery looked at them and said, "I expected to find the two of you otherwise occupied, from what Judge Schofield told me."

"It's damned hard to get very romantic when you're worried about getting killed," said Longarm.

Vickery gave a little shrug. "Well, I'm sorry, but you've missed your opportunity for tonight. You're going back to the jail, Marshal."

"No!" exclaimed Faye.

"I'm afraid so. Marshal Long here will have to spend the rest of the night in the company of Judge Schofield rather than yourself, Mrs. McCormick."

Longarm tasted bitter disappointment in his mouth, not so much because he was going to be separated from Faye—although that was a definite concern—but because they hadn't had a chance to work out a plan to strike back at Vickery. Now, unless he could contrive something else, they wouldn't have that opportunity.

"What's wrong, Colonel?" he asked. "Things aren't going the way you wanted them to?"

"That's not it at all, Longarm," replied Vickery. "I've just decided that I'll feel more comfortable with you locked up behind some solid stone walls and iron bars. I've heard too many stories about how ingenious you are."

"I don't feel too ingenious right about now," Longarm grumbled. He sighed. "Really, what I feel is hungry. You reckon we could get some food over at the jail? I don't figure the judge and me will be sleeping much tonight."

Vickery considered the request for a few seconds, then nodded. "I think that can be arranged. Mrs. McCormick works at the local cafe, I understand. I'll have her bring something over to you."

"Much obliged," Longarm said, being careful not to show his real pleasure at Vickery's decision. The colonel had played right into his hands, and already Longarm had the beginnings of an idea how to take advantage of this opportunity.

Once more, though, he would have to wait for the right moment to make his move. For now, all he could do was stand back as Vickery drew a Colt and ordered him to step over by the windows. The colonel ushered Faye out of the room and said to one of the men outside, "Take Mrs. McCormick over to the cafe. She's going to be fetching a meal to the jail a bit later."

"Yes, sir, Colonel," the owlhoot guard replied crisply.

When Faye was gone—after casting a last glance over her shoulder at Longarm—Vickery gestured with his gun and said, "Now you, Marshal."

Longarm walked out into the corridor, and wasn't surprised to find Major Niland and another four-man escort waiting for him. Vickery obviously considered him a mighty dangerous man. Yet the colonel's self-confidence—so strong that it bordered on arrogance—had so far kept him from disposing of this potential threat.

More than anything else, Longarm realized, Vickery was keeping him alive so that he could lord it over his prisoner and boast about his genius. That was a mistake.

With any luck, before this night was over Vickery would discover just what a bad mistake it had been.

Chapter 10

Major Niland and the other men marched Longarm back down the street to the big stone building, keeping him virtually surrounded just as they had done earlier. The street was still deserted except for Vickery's men.

When they reached the jail, Judge Schofield was still sitting on the cot inside the cell, head down. Lieutenant Carson unlocked the cell door, then stepped back with drawn gun to cover Longarm while the lawman moved inside the bars. Niland's gun was in his hand too. Neither of the outlaws holstered their weapons until Carson had slammed the cell door shut.

"You boys seem to think I'm a ring-tailed terror," Longarm said dryly as he turned to face them.

"We know how to be careful with a prisoner," said Niland. He turned to Carson. "However, the colonel told me you don't have to stand guard here in the cell block anymore, Lieutenant. These men have been thoroughly searched. There's nothing on them they could use to get out of here."

Longarm knew that to be true in his own case. His pockets were completely empty. He assumed the search had been carried out while he was unconscious. As efficient as Vickery's men were, he doubted if Schofield was still carrying anything that could come in handy either.

"You can remain on guard in the office," Niland said to Carson. "But stay alert. The colonel doesn't trust these two."

"Yes, sir," Carson said. "At the first sign of trouble, I'll be back here."

"There has been one other modification to your orders." Niland looked at Longarm and Schofield. "You now have permission to kill them if it becomes necessary."

Carson nodded. He accepted that as easily as he had the previous order about shooting the prisoners in the knee if they caused trouble.

Niland and Carson left the cell block, closing and locking the door to the office behind them. Longarm stood at the bars for a moment, his hands clasped around the iron, then moved over to a corner of the cell. Schofield was studiously ignoring him.

"Anything happen while I was gone, Judge?" asked Longarm as he sank into a cross-legged position on the floor again.

Schofield gave a curt shake of his head. "Nothing except that soulless young man standing there and looking at me like I was some sort of . . . bug."

"The way you looked at the folks Thurgood hauled in front of you on phony charges?"

Schofield heaved a sigh. "If you want to come over here and take your revenge on me, Long, I don't suppose I can stop you. Perhaps I even deserve the grudge you seem to bear against me."

"There's no perhaps about it," Longarm grunted. "You're a crook, Judge, plain and simple."

Schofield made no reply to the accusation.

After a moment, Longarm went on in a quiet voice, "But you're not as bad as that Colonel Vickery."

"The man's a lunatic," said Schofield. "When I looked in his eyes, I saw . . . I saw . . . There was nothing there."

Longarm pretty well agreed with that assessment. He said as much, then went on. "It seems to me that the two of us ought to be thinking about working together, Judge. Vickery's got to be stopped."

90

Schofield's head lifted, and for the first time in a while, he looked straight at Longarm. "But what can we do?" he asked. "We're prisoners. There's no way out of this jail."

"Are you sure about that?"

"I ought to be," Schofield replied with a snort. "I designed it. It's escape-proof."

"Yeah, you wanted to be sure you could keep all those dangerous criminals in here before you shipped 'em off to work in your Mexican pard's silver mine, didn't you?"

Schofield frowned. "It was a legitimate business arrangement, I tell you."

"That's all right, Judge," Longarm said with a wave of his hand. "I reckon we'd better just let that lie for now. It's more important that we come up with some way of spoiling Vickery's plan."

The judge's expression fell again. For a moment, there had been defiance on his bulldog-like face. Now there was only defeat. "I just don't see any way," he muttered as he shook his head.

"Oh? You *like* somebody else riding in and taking over *your* town?"

Longarm saw that his verbal thrust had found its target. Schofield didn't lift his head right away, but his thick fingers clenched into fists.

"I built Inferno," he said after a minute. "This town wouldn't even be here if it wasn't for me. I'm the one who persuaded the railroad to dig a well and put a water stop in this spot."

"Then you've got more reason than anybody to hate Vickery," Longarm pointed out.

Slowly, Judge Schofield nodded. "You're right. I do." He raised his eyes to meet Longarm's gaze. "I can't let him get away with this."

The two of them had just formed an alliance, Longarm realized, no matter how impossible such a thing would have seemed earlier in the day. Schofield was a venal little criminal, and no doubt he had sent innocent men to their deaths in that silver mine across the border. Sooner or later, once the threat of Vickery had been eliminated, Longarm would have to deal with that issue.

But not now. At the moment there were more pressing worries.

"Vickery doesn't plan to let us live," said Longarm. "I'm sure of that. Once he's gotten what he came here for, he'll kill both of us. I wouldn't put it past him to loot the whole town and burn it down around the ears of the citizens."

"But he promised that if we all cooperate . . ." Schofield began.

"And you believed him?" Longarm said scornfully.

"Well . . . not really. I was hoping. . . . " Schofield shook his head. "I know you're right, Marshal. I just didn't want to think about it."

A faint grin tugged at Longarm's mouth. "So you've decided to believe me about being a U.S. deputy marshal."

"Hell, I've known that all along," Schofield admitted. "We found your credentials in your saddlebags, just like you said we would."

Longarm felt his face flush with anger. He had suspected all along that Schofield and Thurgood were aware of his true identity, but to hear the judge confess so brazenly like that . . .

Longarm forced down the reaction, telling himself once again that he could square accounts with Schofield later. Thurgood and the other men involved in the scheme, the town deputies, were already beyond the reach of either justice or vengeance. They had died because they had encountered an even greater evil.

"We're going to have to figure out some way to get out of here," said Longarm, keeping his voice low enough so that Carson couldn't hear it through the thick cell block door. "If we can get our hands on a horse, you can ride for help."

Schofield raised his eyebrows in surprise. "You'd trust me not to just flee and never look back?"

"Like you said, Judge, Inferno is your town. I don't think you'd abandon it."

After a moment, Schofield nodded. "You're right. I wouldn't. But what would you do while I sought assistance?"

"Make life as miserable as possible for Vickery and his bunch, maybe cut down the odds a little." Longarm shrugged. "Maybe try to stir up the townspeople enough for them to pitch in and lend a hand in the fight."

Schofield shook his head. "Oh, no, they'd never do that. I know these people. As long as their own skins are safe, they won't lift a finger to help you or anybody else, Long."

Longarm hated to think he might be right. Too much depended on him getting at least a little help from some outside source. "Could be they'd surprise you," he said. "One of them has already decided she's had enough. She's ready to fight back."

"And who might that be?"

"Faye McCormick."

"The Widow McCormick . . . I knew she had succumbed to your charm, Marshal. I didn't realize you had inspired her to have some gumption as well."

"Most folks do, if you dig deep enough."

Schofield placed his hands on his knees and leaned forward on the cot. "Well. How do you propose that we make our escape from here?"

"We won't be able to fool Carson near as easy as I tricked that deputy who was standing guard earlier," Longarm cautioned.

"Perhaps if we pretended to be fighting, we could lure him into the cell."

Longarm shook his head firmly at that suggestion. "Carson doesn't have to keep us alive. He'd just stand back and watch us kill each other. Either that, or shoot us himself to simplify matters. No, it's got to be something better than that." He paused, then added, "Faye will be here in a little while. We'll talk it over with her."

"Mrs. McCormick is coming here? Why?"

"I talked Vickery into letting us have a little midnight snack. Since I figure it's a little after midnight now, it's overdue."

"Food," said Schofield. "Excellent. I always think better on a full stomach."

Thinking was one thing, Longarm told himself. Fighting was another.

To get out of this mess, it was likely going to take some of both.

Faye arrived not long after that, carrying a large, cloth-covered tray just as she had earlier. Carson removed the cloth from the tray and checked the food much more thoroughly than the deputy had done at supper time. Longarm wasn't surprised when Faye gave him a minuscule shake of her head to indicate that there were no weapons hidden in the meal this time. He hadn't expected her to try to slip something past the lieutenant.

"Can I stay and visit a while?" Faye asked when she had passed the tray through the slot in the bars.

Carson considered for a couple of seconds, then nodded his head. "I suppose so. But I'm going to leave the cell block door open, and I'll be sitting where I can watch you. My eyes will be on you every moment, ma'am, so don't try to pass anything to the prisoners."

"I won't," Faye pledged. "You have my word on that."

Carson went back into the office, leaving the cell block door open as he had said he would, and Faye drew up the stool next to the bars so that she could sit down.

Longarm and Judge Schofield split up the plates of food on the tray and dug in. It was the same fare as earlier, and Longarm suspected it was left over from the supper Claude had fixed at the cafe. But it was still good, and he ate hungrily. After the exhausting day, he needed sustenance if he was to remain awake and alert the rest of the night.

Faye glanced through the open door at Carson, then asked softly, "What are we going to do, Custis? Have you come up with a plan?"

"Maybe the start of one," said Longarm, his own voice so low that it wouldn't carry any farther than Faye's ears. "But it depends on the townspeople. Do you think you could find some of them who'd be willing to help us?"

"You mean for them to storm the jail or something like that?" Faye asked with a frown. "I don't think anybody would do that, Custis. Except maybe me and Claude."

Longarm smiled grimly. "No offense, Faye, but the two of you wouldn't make much of a rescue party. No, what we need is a distraction of some sort, so that when we do bust out of here, we won't run into a bunch of Vickery's men as soon as we set foot outside the building."

"A distraction . . ." Faye repeated. "I might be able to set up something like that."

"Is Vickery still keeping everybody off the street?"

She nodded. "Except for me. He's issued orders that I'm to be allowed to move back and forth between here and the cafe and the hotel."

"Why the hotel?" Longarm asked, puzzled. The jail and the cafe, he could understand, because Faye had delivered this meal to him and Schofield.

She looked down at the floor, and her pretty features grew flushed with embarrassment. "I think . . . I think Vickery has taken a shine to me. He told me to put on my prettiest dress and come back over to his room in the hotel when I got through with this errand."

Longarm's jaw tightened. "That son of a bitch," he muttered under his breath.

Schofield put a hand on Longarm's arm. "Take it easy, Marshal," he advised, low-voiced. "This is a good thing. Mrs. McCormick here has succeeded in infiltrating the enemy camp."

Longarm looked impatient as he said, "Vickery doesn't trust her. You ought to know that."

"No, he doesn't trust me," Faye said quickly, "but he's interested in me, and that's enough. It's given me more freedom of movement." She shrugged. "If I have to give myself to him, well, I figure it's worth it."

Part of Longarm's brain rebelled strongly at that notion, but the more logical parts accepted it as inevitable. If nothing else, his years of chasing owlhoots and badmen of all stripes had taught him that sometimes a fella had to be pragmatic about things. He nodded and said, "All right. But I don't have to like it."

Faye leaned closer to him, again glancing toward Carson before she did so. "What do you want me to do?"

His own voice a whisper, Longarm said, "All right, this is the way we'll work it. . . . ."

After a few more minutes, Carson came into the cell block and said to the prisoners, "Are you finished eating?"

Longarm and Schofield were just scraping up the last of the gravy from the roast beef with their biscuits. Longarm put the bite in his mouth, chewed, swallowed, and nodded. "The condemned men ate a hearty last meal," he said dryly.

"You won't be harmed if you don't cause any trouble," Carson snapped. The words sounded hollow, and everyone in the cell block knew it. There was no way Vickery was going to leave behind a judge and a U.S. marshal after whatever he had planned for the following morning.

"Put your forks and the plates back on the tray," Carson went on. "Don't try to hide anything."

"Wouldn't think of it," said Schofield. He did as Carson had ordered, and so did Longarm, who passed the tray back through the bars to Faye. As she took it, Carson looked carefully at the tray, to make sure everything that had gone into the cell was coming back out except the food which had been eaten. The outlaw lieutenant nodded, satisfied that none of them were trying to trick him in any fashion.

He stepped back so that Faye could precede him out of the cell block. While Carson was still within easy earshot, Longarm yawned and said, "That meal made me sleepy. Reckon I'll rest until morning."

"I believe I'll retire for the night as well," said Schofield.

Carson glanced back at them, a slight frown of suspicion on his face. There was nothing unusual about someone being tired when it was well after midnight, however. Schofield stretched out on the cot and wrapped the thin blanket around himself. Longarm sat down on the floor beside the wall again, stretched his legs out in front of him, crossed his arms over his chest, and leaned back, his eyes drooping closed.

Carson gave a little shrug and followed Faye out of the cell block.

Longarm heard the front door of the sheriff's office open and close. Faye was gone again, out there in the middle of the now-hostile town, and riding on her were all of their hopes for surviving this mess. It was up to her now. Longarm hoped she was up to the task.

A faint smile touched his lips as he pretended to doze. For a long time following the death of her husband, Faye had been in a sort of waking sleep, content to go from day to day without really caring about anything.

But Longarm's arrival in Inferno, coupled with the ordeal that had begun soon after, had awakened Faye from her mental and spiritual slumber. Her eyes were wide open and looking to the future. She could see what she wanted.

And Longarm had sensed that she was willing to fight to get it.

Now, if she could only convince some of the other good folks of Inferno to go along with her . . .

Chapter 11

Faye McCormick was still as frightened as she had ever been in her life, but she had grown accustomed to the fear by now. It was always there in the back of her mind and in the pit of her stomach, but she was able to accept it and move on. Like the dull ache of a bad tooth, she just ignored the fear as much as possible. Custis Long was counting on her.

The whole blasted town was counting on her, when you came right down to it, whether the citizens of Inferno knew it or not.

The guard who had followed her from the hotel to the cafe to the jail was waiting for her at the front door of the big stone building. He reminded her a little of Lieutenant Carson, in that he was young and earnest and stony-faced. But he was a little taller than Carson and had dark hair instead of blond. Faye didn't know his name and didn't ask what it was.

"I have to take this tray back over to the cafe," she told him, "and then I'm supposed to stop by my house before I go back to the hotel."

"Yes, ma'am," said the guard with a nod. "Major Niland gave me my orders, ma'am."

Faye suppressed the irritation and frustration she felt. How could such a polite, nice-looking young man be part

99

of a vicious, murdering outlaw gang? Yet there was no doubt that was what Vickery's bunch was. It just goes to show you, she decided, that looks don't really count for much. What a person did was the true measure of their worth.

And this young man would gun her down without mercy if she tried to run away from him. She was certain of that.

Only one lamp was burning in the cafe, which had effectively closed for business as soon as Vickery and his advance squad had ridden into town. Claude was waiting there for Faye, sitting on one of the stools in front of the counter and nervously rubbing his hands together. He stood up and took the tray from her as she came up to him, trailed by the guard.

"Are you all right, Faye?" he asked anxiously.

She nodded. "I'm fine. Don't worry about me, Claude."

"None of those guards have mistreated you, have they?"

"Of course not. We're all cooperating with them, remember?"

Her back was to the guard, so he couldn't see her face as she dropped one eyelid in a wink to the old cafe owner. She had to let Claude know that cooperation with the invaders was the last thing she really had in mind.

She thought she saw the light of understanding in his rheumy eyes. He turned and put the tray on the counter with a clatter. "You better run along home now," he told her as he swung back toward her. "I'll walk you."

"The lady already has an escort," the guard put in curtly from the doorway.

Claude snorted. "If you're worried about me, young feller, you can guard me too. My house is right close to Faye's. This gal's like a daughter to me, and I want to make sure she gets home all right."

Faye turned toward the guard. "Please." She took hold of Claude's arm. "He's such an old dear."

Claude grinned, going along with the act. He was actually about the most irascible old coot Faye had ever run into, and more than once she had regretted going to work for him. But for now, the important thing was for both of them to appear as harmless as possible.

The guard shrugged. "I suppose it wouldn't hurt anything. Come on, mister."

Claude blew out the lantern and went to the door with Faye. She still had hold of his arm. They moved off down the street toward her house, trailed closely by the guard, who kept his hand on the butt of his gun. As they passed some of the other sentries Vickery had set out, the young man called softly to them to let them know it was all right for Faye and Claude to be abroad in the night. Otherwise, Faye and Claude would have been shot on sight.

"That's my shack right there," Claude told the guard as they passed a small adobe hut about fifty yards from Faye's house.

"All right, go on inside and stay there," said the young man. "Don't poke your head out before we're gone tomorrow, or you're liable to get it shot off."

Claude chuckled. "I'll remember that, young feller. I sure will."

Faye and the guard moved on toward her house as Claude turned toward the adobe hut. The old man took only a couple of steps in that direction before he halted abruptly and whirled back toward the others. He clenched his hands together and swung his clubbed fists at the back of the guard's head.

The man must have heard the sudden rush of Claude's footsteps, because he started to turn around. Claude slammed into him, the blow awkward but powerful enough to knock him off balance. Faye had been waiting for something to happen, and when the guard stumbled against her, her hands darted out and closed over the butt of his holstered gun. She jerked the revolver from leather and raised it, smashing it into the side of the guard's head as hard as she could. She didn't want to fire a shot. The sounds of a scuffle like this were risky enough.

The guard went to his knees with a groan. His hat had fallen off when Faye hit him, so she could see his head clearly in the starlight. She swung the gun again, putting all the power she could behind the blow. This time there was a dull cracking sound as the barrel of the gun struck the guard's skull. He pitched over onto his side and lay motionless.

Faye was breathing hard, and a ball of sickness was rolling around in her belly. She knew there was a good chance she had killed the young man with that second blow. There was no time now to worry about such things, however. Claude bent over, grabbed the guard's shoulders, and dragged him over into the shadow of the adobe shack.

"Lord, girl, I didn't know you could move so fast and nasty," he said. "If I had, I might not've given you such a hard time at the cafe."

"Don't worry about it, Claude," Faye told him. "Is he—?"

"Dead, or the next thing to it," the old man confirmed. "Was I supposed to jump him like that? I couldn't quite figure out what you had in mind."

"That was fine, just fine," she said, forcing down the nausea that threatened to well up inside her. "We're far enough away from the other guards that I don't think any of them saw anything. I've got to go on to my house now, though. Vickery's expecting me back at the hotel once I've changed my clothes."

"What? Shoot, Faye, you can't—"

"Don't argue with me about this, Claude," she said firmly. "You and I both have a job to do. Can you slip along the backs of the buildings and talk to some of the other people in town? Marshal Long needs a distraction about an hour from now. He thought maybe if some of you could shoot your guns off in the air and draw Vickery's guards away from the other end of town, he and the judge could get out of the jail."

Claude rubbed his beard-stubbled jaw. "I don't know. If we start a ruckus, that feller who calls himself a colonel is liable to have us all shot."

"We have to take a chance, so that the marshal can stop whatever Vickery has planned for in the morning. It's something to do with the westbound train."

"Figures to loot it, more'n likely," Claude decided. He took a deep breath. "All right, Faye. I'll do what I can. I never really believed that bastard when he said nobody else would be hurt anyway. Killin' comes too danged easy to him."

"Can you move around town without the guards seeing you?"

Claude snorted. "Hell, I fought the Apaches up in the Superstitions twenty years ago. If I can dodge them, I can sneak past a bunch of no-account owlhoots."

Faye put a hand on his stringy old arm and squeezed. "Thanks, Claude. Be careful."

He chuckled and said, "Shoot, this might even be fun."

Faye left him there and hurried on to her house. She still had the rest of her part in Longarm's plan to carry out.

Back in the jail, Judge Schofield was snoring loudly as he slept on the cot. As it turned out, the judge wasn't being forced to feign slumber. He had actually dozed off, which was fine with Longarm. The snores sounded real because they were authentic, and the sound made an excellent cover for what Longarm was doing. Schofield could sure saw wood once he got going, Longarm thought as he ripped another piece off the blanket he had taken from the cot before the judge fell asleep.

Longarm wasn't sure how well this was going to work, but a man sometimes had to make do with what he had. In this case, it was a ratty old blanket that had been washed so many times it wasn't much thicker than a sheet. Longarm was tearing it into long, narrow strips, starting each of them by gnawing on the edge of the blanket with his teeth. The slight sounds the blanket made as it tore were masked by Schofield's stentorian snoring.

As long as the judge was making such a racket, Longarm felt fairly confident Lieutenant Carson would stay in the sheriff's office. Carson would be able to hear the snoring, even through the cell block door, and would know that Schofield was still there. Longarm was quieter, but every so often as he worked on the blanket, he let out a snort and a

103

mutter like a sleeping man rolling over, just in case Carson was listening closer than he expected.

In the middle of the night like this, without a good view of the stars, it was difficult to tell exactly how much time was passing. Longarm wasn't sure how long he and Schofield had been locked up here. He thought dawn was still a few hours away, but he couldn't be sure of that. Nor did he know exactly when the distraction Faye had promised him would take place—or even *if* it would take place.

All he could do was hope . . . and be ready to make his move when the time came.

Finally, he had a pile of blanket strips on the floor beside him. He began tying the strips together, end to end, making the knots as tight and strong as possible. When he had several longer segments completed, he started weaving them together, braiding them like a Mexican reata. Those rawhide ropes were incredibly strong. He couldn't hope for such strength from this makeshift rope fashioned out of an old blanket, but it would have to do. And his aim would have to be true, because he would likely get only one chance to dab a loop on his target.

Longarm stood up and went to the cell's single window, taking the blanket-rope with him. He looked up at the stars, trying to judge from their position in the sky what the time was. Surely more than an hour had passed since Faye had left the jail, he thought. He turned away from the window and went to the bunk, where he knelt and put a hand on Schofield's shoulder.

"Eh!" The judge started up violently. "What—"

"Take it easy, Schofield," hissed Longarm. "We don't want to spook the lieutenant just yet. But any time now, we'll have a chance to make our move." He hoped the confident words weren't just empty, wishful thinking.

That was when a fusillade of gunshots suddenly slammed through the night.

Couldn't get any better timing than that, Longarm thought as he stood up sharply, swung away from the bunk, and turned toward the bars. He shook out a loop in the rope and held it slightly behind him, where Carson wouldn't be likely to see it right away from the cell block corridor. Behind Longarm, Schofield came to his feet as well.

Shots were still coming from the other end of town. When Longarm listened closely, he could hear men yelling too. Obviously, Faye had been successful in at least part of her mission.

With the pounding of hurried footsteps, Lieutenant Carson threw the cell block door open and burst into the corridor. The young outlaw was running true to the form Longarm had expected. With trouble breaking out elsewhere in Inferno, Carson was moving to stand a closer guard on his prisoners. It was typical military thinking. Carson's hand was on the butt of his pistol, but he hadn't drawn the gun yet. He was just about to slide it from its holster when the marshal's arm snaked between the bars, bringing the loop of makeshift rope with it. With a flick of his wrist, Longarm sent the loop sailing at Carson.

It was a good thing that throwing a rope was one of those skills a fella never completely forgot. Longarm had made thousands of such throws during his cowboying days, and the instincts were still there in his muscles and tendons and sinews. The loop snapped open as it came out of the shadows, and before Carson had a chance to avoid it, the rope had settled past his head and shoulders and around his upper arms. Longarm jerked the loop closed.

Carson let out a startled yell as Longarm yanked him toward the bars with all the strength in his powerful, rangy form. The rope held, for which Longarm was profoundly grateful. He'd have looked damned silly standing there holding part of the rope while Carson was still free. That silly look would have lasted about two seconds, and then the lieutenant would have probably shot him.

Instead, Carson slammed headfirst into the bars, and as he did so, Judge Schofield lunged forward, reaching through the openings between the bars. He grabbed Carson's coat with a death-grip and kept the outlaw from bouncing back due to the impact. In fact, Schofield was able to pull him hard against the bars a second time.

By then, Longarm had dropped the rope and was reaching through the bars himself. He plucked Carson's gun from its holster and whipped it up in a backhanded blow that caught the guard on the jaw. Carson sagged in Schofield's grip, out cold.

"Hang on to him, Judge," Longarm warned.

"Don't worry, he's not going anywhere," Schofield said.

Longarm tucked the pistol behind his belt, then reached through the bars again and worked the ring of keys loose from Carson's belt. He hurried over to the door and quickly found the key that turned the lock. The door swung open, and Longarm and Schofield were free.

"You can let go of him now," Longarm said, and when Schofield did so, Carson slumped senselessly to the floor of the corridor. Longarm stepped out of the cell, followed closely by the judge. He bent over Carson long enough to unbuckle the lieutenant's shell belt and holster, then strapped it around his own hips. Longarm slid the Colt back into leather. It wasn't like his usual cross-draw rig, but he could manage well enough.

"There are more weapons in the sheriff's office," said Schofield. "We'd best arm ourselves well."

Longarm nodded as he moved past Carson's unconscious body. He was aware that the shooting in the other part of town had stopped. He wasn't sure what that meant, other than the fact that Vickery's guards might not be as preoccupied as he would have liked while he and Schofield were making their escape from the jail.

And there was Faye to worry about too. Longarm couldn't help but wonder where she was now, and if she was safe.

Chapter 12

The red dress Faye wore had been packed away carefully among her things when she and her husband started west. Since then, she had never had an occasion to wear it. Truth be told, she hadn't worn it much before her husband's death either. It was too daring, with the neckline plummeting like it did deep into the creamy valley between her breasts, and the color of the dress itself made her look a little like a fallen woman, Faye was convinced.

But as she glanced at herself briefly in the mirror over the dressing table in her bedroom, then paused for a longer look, she had to admit that the dress looked good on her—and she looked good in it. She brushed her chestnut hair back from shoulders that were left mostly bare by the gown.

Not bad for somebody who had just killed a man a few minutes earlier, she mused.

With a sigh, she forced that bitter thought from her mind. She had done only what she had been forced to do under the circumstances. She hadn't really meant to kill the guard either. Knocking him unconscious would have been enough.

Besides, she sure as blazes hadn't asked Vickery and his gang of outlaws to ride in here and take over Inferno and put the lives of all its citizens in danger. The man she had killed had to bear some of the blame for his own fate.

She was sick and tired of feeling guilty, damn it.

With a toss of her head, she left the bedroom, draped a shawl around her shoulders, and went out of the house into the night, which had finally started to cool off. In fact, as the air hit her bare skin, which there was more of than usual, a little shiver went through her.

Of course, that might have been from fear as much as anything, she thought. . . .

Boldness was the order of the day now. She marched back up the street, and when she encountered the first of the sentries Vickery had posted, she called out softly, "Please don't shoot! It's me—Mrs. McCormick. I came by here just a little while ago."

The outlaw had brought his rifle to his shoulder, but he lowered it a little as he asked, "Where's Sergeant Dawes?"

"The guard who was with me, you mean?"

"That's right. My orders are to shoot any unaccompanied civilians on sight. That would be you, ma'am."

"The sergeant . . . Dawes, did you say his name was? He saw someone trying to slip out of town and went after them. He said I could come back up here and get you to take me to the hotel. Colonel Vickery is expecting me."

Faye kept her voice level and under control, although she allowed the nervousness that would be normal in this situation to creep through her words. If this man didn't believe her story, he might take her back to her house and go looking for the dead Sergeant Dawes. That could prove disastrous.

"So that's what Dawes said, is it?"

Faye nodded. "That's right."

"And I guess he told you my name, since I'm supposed to take you back to the hotel."

Faye swallowed hard and cast her memory back over the walk she had taken down this street not long before, when Dawes had brought her and Claude from the cafe. Dawes had called some of the other guards by name, she remembered, but had this man been one of them? And if so, could she dredge the correct name out of her memory?

"Of course he did, so I'd be sure to talk to the right man. You're Sergeant Mitchum."

It was little more than a shot in the dark, but the sentry grunted and lowered his rifle the rest of the way. "I guess it's all right, then," he said. "Come on. You're going to the hotel, you said?"

"That's right."

Mitchum chuckled. "Got to give the colonel credit. He knows a beautiful woman when he sees one."

Faye forced herself to smile. "Why, thank you, Sergeant."

Mitchum fell in step beside her as they started along the street. "You say Dawes saw somebody sneaking around and went after them?"

"That's right."

"Haven't heard any shooting," muttered the outlaw. "Reckon Dawes hasn't found whoever he saw. But he will. You folks ought to have better sense than to disobey orders."

"Most of us are trying to cooperate," said Faye. "I certainly am."

"I'm sure the colonel appreciates that."

Nothing more was said between them as they proceeded to the hotel. Mitchum called out to the other guards along the way, just as Dawes had done on the way down the street. When they reached the hotel, the bearded owlhoot called Major Niland greeted them.

"The colonel is waiting for the woman," Niland said as Faye and Mitchum stepped into the lobby. "Where's Dawes?"

"She claims he saw someone sneaking around and went after them," Mitchum said with a nod toward Faye.

"Is that true?" Niland snapped, his intense gaze fastened on her.

"Yes, it is," she lied easily. "Your Sergeant Dawes thought some of the townspeople might be up to something."

"I'd better go check on him," Niland said, not looking happy about this development.

Quickly, Mitchum said, "I would have, sir, but I didn't think the young lady ought to be wandering around alone.

One of the men might have shot her by mistake.''

"If there was a mistake made, it was by her," said Niland. "Let me take her up to the colonel, and then we'll go see if we can find Dawes. I've got a bad feeling about this."

Faye didn't like hearing that. Obviously, Niland suspected she wasn't telling the truth. She didn't want the major's heightened sense of alertness leading him to Claude and anyone else the old cafe owner could enlist to thwart this owlhoot gang.

But there was nothing she could do or say without risking increasing Niland's suspicions that much more, so she kept quiet. Niland took hold of her arm and led her up the stairs, none too gently. When they reached the door of the room Colonel Vickery had commandeered, Niland knocked on it and called out, "It's Major Niland, sir. Mrs. McCormick is here."

"Excellent," said Vickery's voice from inside. "Bring her in."

The colonel had removed his coat, she saw as she entered the room, but he still wore his vest. He was smoking a cigar, and on a side table was a bottle and a couple of glasses. She saw Niland glance at the bottle and glasses in what seemed to be surprise. Evidently the colonel wasn't much of a drinking man.

Which meant Vickery considered this a special occasion. Faye didn't really like the thought of that.

Vickery nodded curtly to Niland and said, "That will be all, Major."

"Yes, sir," replied Niland. "Sir?"

"Yes, what is it?" Vickery sounded impatient, and he hadn't taken his eyes off Faye since she came into the room.

"Sir, there's been a report that some of the civilians are disobeying orders and venturing out of their houses. According to Mrs. McCormick, Sergeant Dawes abandoned the duty he had been assigned and went in pursuit of an unidentified civilian."

Finally, Vickery looked at his second in command. "Abandoned his duty?" he echoed. "That's not like Dawes."

110

"No, sir, it's not," agreed Niland. Once more he glanced suspiciously at Faye.

She tried not to let her heart sink. The story she had hastily spun might not hold water with these men, in which case they could try to force the truth out of her. Vickery was undeniably taken with her, but she didn't believe for an instant that the man would allow passion to interfere with accomplishing his greater goal.

"Find Dawes," Vickery ordered after a moment. "I want to hear his explanation for this directly from him."

"Yes, sir."

"I'll keep an eye on Mrs. McCormick while you're gone," said Vickery. "And if you find that the townspeople *are* up to something . . . kill them."

Faye repressed a shudder at the coldness in Vickery's tone.

"Yes, sir," Niland responded, sounding a bit more enthusiastic now. The man was bloodthirsty, Faye thought, and she hated to consider what he might do to her if he discovered her part in what had happened to Dawes. Not to mention what Vickery might do . . .

For the moment, however, she was safe. Niland left the room and closed the door behind him. Vickery moved over to the side table and asked smoothly, "Would you like a drink, Mrs. McCormick? I had this whiskey and these glasses brought up from the hotel's barroom. Normally I don't allow any drinking, on my part or on the part of my men, while we're carrying out a mission, but I thought that tonight was a little different."

"Oh?" Faye forced herself to say. "And why is that?"

The colonel smiled at her. "Because I'm with you, of course, dear lady. I thought a drink might make you more . . . comfortable."

"I could use one, all right," she admitted with a sigh.

Vickery pulled the cork in the whiskey bottle and splashed some of the amber liquid in each glass. He picked up both of them and carried them over to Faye. She took one from him, and he held up his glass.

"To the success of the mission," he said.

Faye couldn't make herself drink to that, so she said instead, "To tonight." That was vague enough, and promising enough, to satisfy Vickery.

He clinked his glass against hers, then threw back the liquor. Faye drank hers more slowly. She had never really cared for the taste of whiskey, but she had to admit that the warmth that spread through her from her belly had a bracing effect on her nerves. She didn't quite feel like she was about to jump out of her skin anymore.

Vickery reached toward the bottle. "Would you like another?"

Faye shook her head. She couldn't take a chance on her mind getting too muddled. She had to stay alert. There was no way of knowing how soon the distraction staged by Claude and his friends would occur.

"I'm glad you've decided to be reasonable," Vickery went on. "It makes things much more pleasant when there's not a lot of trouble."

"Why wouldn't I be reasonable?" asked Faye. "Whatever it is that brought you here to Inferno, it's none of my business."

"But you'd probably like to know why we've come here, wouldn't you?"

She shrugged, noting the way his gaze lingered on her mostly bare shoulders. "I'm curious," she admitted. "Who wouldn't be?" If he was in an expansive mood and wanted to talk for a while, she definitely wanted to encourage him. More knowledge concerning his plans might come in handy later, and besides, as long as he was talking, his mind wouldn't be on doing anything else.

Vickery chuckled. "A good commander is wise to keep his own counsel," he said, "but I must admit, I'm rather proud of this operation. It's going to make me a very rich man, and the United States government will learn that they made a terrible mistake when they forced me to resign my commission."

That part about the government was puzzling to Faye. Custis Long thought that Vickery planned to rob the west-bound train when it stopped for water around dawn, and

Claude had shared that opinion. Vickery was talking like it was more than a simple train robbery he had in mind, though. Carefully, Faye said, "The government makes a lot of mistakes, I suppose."

Vickery's fingers tightened on the glass in his hand. He filled it with whiskey again and drained it. "They claimed I was a bad officer," he said bitterly, his good mood vanishing before Faye's eyes. "All because of a simple mistake."

He fell silent, so Faye took a chance on prodding him a little. "Was it something that happened in . . . combat?" She could imagine him being cashiered out of the army because some error in tactics had cost the lives of his troops.

Vickery shook his head. "They claimed I lost eighty-seven thousand dollars."

"Lost?" Faye repeated. "Do you mean they accused you of stealing—"

He didn't let her finish the question. "No, the money was lost through bookkeeping errors. At least that was the finding of the court-martial panel." Vickery snorted in contempt. "The money probably *was* stolen, but by some congressman or senator. I know it never reached my unit for disbursement."

"You were . . . a bookkeeper?"

"Paymaster," snapped Vickery.

A bookkeeper, Faye thought to herself. Vickery hadn't even been a field commander. He had been a desk soldier, a pencil pusher, and yet he had come riding into Inferno and taken over the town like he was Custer or Sherman or U.S. Grant.

And they had let him do it.

It was all Faye could do not to laugh out loud, and the next instant, she wanted to cry. All of this had happened because some disgruntled former bureaucrat wanted to pretend to be some sort of dashing cavalry officer. Obviously, Vickery played the part well.

And equally obviously, he was insane. There was no telling what sort of grandiose scheme he had hatched. But there had to be the promise of a big payoff in it; otherwise the

113

rest of the outlaws wouldn't have played along with his military notions.

Faye swallowed hard and said, "Well, I'm sure the government will regret what they did to you, all right. How . . . how are you going to show them what a mistake they made?"

Vickery's mood improved now that he sensed another opportunity to boast. He put the cigar back in his mouth, grinned around it, and asked, "Have you ever heard of the Gadsden Purchase?"

Faye frowned. "Well . . . maybe. It had something to do with the United States buying land from Mexico."

Vickery pointed at the floor under his feet, and by extension, the ground underneath the hotel. "This land," he said. "The southern part of Arizona Territory. The United States bought it from Mexico in 1854. But there were little things in the purchase treaty that didn't satisfy either side. There always are. And every time a new government comes into power south of the border—which is about every year or so, it seems like—some items have to be hashed out all over again. So even though it's been over twenty-five years since the treaty was signed and this part of the country became U.S. territory, negotiations between our government and Mexico have continued." He puffed on the cigar and then blew smoke toward the ceiling. "Now they think they finally have everything worked out."

"They do?"

Vickery nodded solemnly. "That's why William A. Wheeler is coming to Inferno."

"William A. Wheeler," repeated Faye. The name sounded vaguely familiar to her, but she couldn't place it. She started to frown. Then she gasped suddenly as she remembered just who William A. Wheeler was. "The Vice President?"

"That's right," Vickery said smugly. "He's coming to sign some agreements with representatives of the Mexican government. The meeting is supposed to be a secret, so someone in Washington picked an out-of-the-way place for it. A place where there was a railroad, but close enough to

114

the border for the Mexicans to reach it easily too.''

"Inferno," said Faye.

"Exactly. Vice President Wheeler will be on the train that stops here in a few hours. The Mexican representative will be arriving about the same time by coach. Neither man will have a large force guarding him, since no trouble is expected and neither government wants to call much attention to this meeting.''

Faye put a hand to her mouth. ''Dear Lord! You're going to kidnap the Vice President of the United States!''

"I certainly am," said Vickery, so pleased with himself that he looked fit to bust.

"You're crazy!"

The words came out of Faye's mouth before she could stop them, no matter how much she regretted them an instant later. Vickery's look of self-satisfaction vanished in a flash, and he reached out to grab her upper arms.

"Crazy, am I! You won't think so when I collect a fortune in ransom from both the U.S. and Mexico. They'll pay up, or I'll kill Wheeler and the Mexican representative. Nobody's going to be laughing at me then, or spreading lies and rumors about me! They'll all see that I should have been given a real command, not stuck behind a desk in Washington—''

He broke off suddenly and jerked Faye against him. His mouth came down on hers. She put her hands against his chest and pushed as hard as she could, tearing herself out of his grasp. She staggered back, an unconcealed look of revulsion and anger on her face.

"You're just like all the rest," Vickery said as he glared accusingly at her, breathing heavily. "You've been laughing at me too. But I'll show you . . . I'll show all of you. . . . ''

He lunged toward her, arms outstretched to grab her. Faye tried to twist away, but he was too fast for her. He snagged her arm again and hauled her around to face him. She screamed as he lifted his other hand, ready to slash it down across her face in a brutal slap.

And then, through the open windows of the hotel room, came the sound of all hell breaking loose down the street.

Chapter 13

Longarm felt a little better with a spare six-gun tucked behind his belt and a fully loaded Winchester in his hands. The fact that the shooting down the street had stopped after only a few minutes worried him, and he was anxious to get outside the building as soon as possible. He motioned for Schofield to follow him as he went out of the sheriff's office into the broad main corridor.

The judge had armed himself with a pistol and a shotgun, explaining as he picked up the Greener, "My eyes aren't what they once were. Be glad you're still a young man, Long."

"I just hope we both get a mite older," Longarm said as he led the way out of the sheriff's office. He moved in a half-crouch, ready for trouble.

It wasn't long in coming. The double doors at the main entrance of the big stone building slammed open, and several men came running through. Longarm didn't recognize any of them, but he didn't have to in order to know they were some of Vickery's men. The neat, uniform-like range clothes told him that much.

That, and the way they started shooting at him and Schofield.

Longarm didn't want to waste the cartridges in the Winchester. It would be better to save the long gun for later. So he grabbed the Colt on his hip and blazed away at the outlaws as he flung himself across the corridor toward a closed door. With a crash, the door gave way as Longarm's shoulder rammed into it. He half-fell, half-stumbled into another office of some sort.

Catching his balance, he used the doorway for cover and threw more lead down the hall toward the knot of men just inside the entrance. There was no place for them to hide, so some of them began ducking back out through the still-open doors. Longarm yelled across the corridor to the judge, "Schofield! Come on!"

Schofield darted out from the sheriff's office and started across the hall, taking advantage of the covering fire Longarm was laying down. Longarm had the second pistol out by now and was using it, having emptied the first one. Return fire came from Vickery's men, but the slugs peppered the floor and walls around the judge without hitting him.

Suddenly, Longarm caught a flicker of movement from the corner of his eye, and looked around to see Lieutenant Carson looming up in the door of the sheriff's office, right behind Schofield. Carson had a shotgun in his hands, obviously liberated from the racks in Thurgood's office, like the one Schofield was holding. The young outlaw was swinging the twin barrels up to bear on Schofield's back.

Longarm didn't hesitate. He snapped up the gun in his left hand and fired past Schofield's head, making the judge's eyes widen in shock. The bullet bored into Carson's chest before the outlaw could squeeze the triggers of the scattergun. Carson was thrown backward by the impact of the slug, and both barrels of the shotgun went off as his finger clenched involuntarily on the triggers. The double charge of buckshot went harmlessly into the ceiling and upper part of the opposite wall.

Schofield stumbled into the other office with Longarm, who had already spotted a window across the room. "Go!" shouted Longarm, pointing to the window. "And don't bother opening it!" He tucked away both pistols and snatched up the Winchester, which he had placed on a nearby desk.

"Through the window?" Schofield asked dubiously.

Longarm bit back a curse. There was no time to argue. He took a couple of quick, running steps, ducked his head, and launched himself in a dive that sent him through the closed window in an exploding shower of glass shards and splintered frame.

The drop to the ground was no more than six feet, but Longarm landed awkwardly and fell hard on his left shoulder. He rolled and came up grimacing at the pain shooting down his left arm. He could tell he wasn't seriously hurt, and this was no time to worry about minor injuries.

Schofield appeared in the open window above him and jumped. His landing was even worse than Longarm's, and he was limping when he got to his feet. Longarm bit back a curse. Schofield was going to slow him down, but he couldn't abandon the judge. Not yet anyway. He wanted to see Schofield on a horse, galloping out of Inferno on the way to the next town to fetch help.

A couple of men came running around the front corner of the building, more than likely some of the bunch that had come in the front door and started shooting at Longarm and Schofield. Longarm threw the Winchester to his shoulder and fired at the shadowy figure in the lead. The man went flying backward as if somebody had jerked him with a rope, and his companion dove for cover. Longarm levered another shell into the chamber of the rifle, then grabbed Schofield's arm. "Come on!" he urged.

They ran toward the back of the building. Now that the distraction on the other end of town had been dealt with, more and more of Vickery's men would be converging on this part of Inferno with each passing moment. Longarm wanted to find a horse in a hurry.

Slugs kicked up dust behind their feet as they rounded the rear corner of the building. Longarm didn't bother returning the fire. He just hurried Schofield along as fast as he could. The judge was panting breathlessly, unaccustomed to this much action and exertion.

"There'll be horses in the stable behind the hotel," Longarm said as they ran. "We've got to reach it!"

"Find some . . . closer . . . closer than that!" gasped Schofield. "Over there!" He waved his hand at the dark bulk of another building set behind one of the stores along the street. "Freight wagons! Teams there!" Schofield choked out.

Draft horses wouldn't be very fast, thought Longarm, but they were better than nothing. And there was no guarantee he and Schofield would find anything else. He veered toward the barn, pulling the judge with him.

Before they could reach the barn, shots racketed behind them, and a couple of slugs whined past Longarm's head. He had to angle back to his left, away from the freight barn. Schofield careened along beside him, almost out of control. Longarm expected Schofield to fall down at any moment.

Somehow, Schofield managed to stay on his feet. Longarm studied the rear of the buildings as best he could in the darkness, and decided that they were closer to the hotel than he had thought. They might be able to reach it after all. He hustled Schofield along.

A shot came from Longarm's left. A glance in that direction told him that they were passing a narrow alleyway between a couple of Inferno's buildings. Men were coming down that alley, firing as they came. Longarm shoved Schofield on toward the hotel, then went to one knee and sent three shots screaming down the alley from the Winchester. In such close quarters, it was almost impossible to miss. Men tumbled off their feet, and a high, thin shriek of pain split the night.

Longarm surged to his feet and ran on, confident that he had slowed down the pursuit, at least for a moment or two. But then he heard the boom of Schofield's scattergun, and looked up to see the judge confronting a man who had cut him off from the hotel. Flame blossomed from the gun the man was holding, and Longarm saw Schofield's body jerk under the impact of a slug. Then the second barrel of the shotgun cut down the man as Schofield squeezed the trigger.

Longarm caught up to the judge and grasped his arm. "You all right?" he asked urgently.

"Son of a bitch put a hole in my left arm!" Schofield said. "But I'll be all right . . . if the hole doesn't leak too much blood."

"Come on," Longarm told him. "We're almost at the hotel."

Indeed, the livery barn behind the hotel was only a few yards away now. They had made it, despite the odds.

"When we get inside, we'll get you on a horse," Longarm said as he continued urging the wounded Schofield toward the barn. "You've got to make it to the next town and send some help back here."

"I'll do it," grunted Schofield. "Damned if I won't."

Longarm grabbed the door of the barn and swung it open.

That was when he heard a sound that made his blood turn to ice in his veins. It came from an open window on the second floor of the hotel, and it was faint and muffled, as if it originated in the front of the building, where the room Vickery had taken over was located. The sound was a woman's terrified scream.

Faye.

When the first shots rang out down the street, Vickery froze, his arm still upraised to strike Faye. He stood like that for a moment, then with a snarl shoved her away from him. She tripped and fell, landing on the bed. Her heart was pounding furiously in her chest in a mixture of fear and anger as she looked up at him.

Vickery swung away from her and went to the window, pulling the gun from his holster as he did so. He thrust the gauzy curtain aside and leaned out, peering into the night.

Faye wished that a stray shot would hit him in the head and bore right through that crazed brain of his.

A bit startled that she could even have such a brutal thought, she sat up on the bed and saw that her fervent hope wasn't going to come true. Vickery straightened and stepped back from the window. "There's some trouble at the other end of town," he said. "Some of the civilians must have decided that they have a little backbone after all. But it won't take long for my men to put down this uprising."

She hoped Claude and his friends were all right, but she knew it was likely some of them had been hurt, maybe even killed. Now that she knew what Vickery's plan really involved, she understood how important it was that he be stopped. But that didn't mean she wouldn't mourn for anyone who lost their lives trying to stop him.

Vickery paced back and forth restlessly as the shooting continued, and Faye got the impression he wished he could be in the thick of the battle. The firing died away after a few minutes, and Vickery nodded in satisfaction. "We should hear what happened soon."

Momentarily, footsteps sounded in the hall outside, and a sharp knocking came on the door. Vickery strode over to it and flung it open, revealing the bearded Major Niland.

"Report, Major," snapped Vickery.

"Some old-timers bushwhacked one of the sentries," Niland said. "I'm afraid Private Hobart was killed."

Vickery waved a hand, obviously not too concerned over the fate of the luckless Private Hobart. "How did our men respond?"

"Quickly and efficiently, Colonel. Two of the townsmen who attacked Hobart were killed, and the others were taken prisoner."

Faye's heart sank sickeningly. She couldn't help but wonder if Claude was one of the two men who had been killed.

"Shall we execute the prisoners immediately, Colonel?" Niland went on to ask.

Vickery hesitated for a moment as he frowned in thought; then he shook his head. "Not yet. We'll dispose of them in the morning, after we've captured the Vice President and the Mexican. That will help convince the emissaries we send back to their respective governments that we mean business. For the time being, just keep the prisoners under close guard."

"Yes, sir," replied Niland with a nod. He paused, then added, "I have one more item to report, Colonel. The body of Sergeant Dawes has been found."

"Dawes!" exclaimed Vickery. He turned his head to look at Faye, who had stood up and retreated to the far side of the bed, where she waited with her arms crossed in front of her, rubbing her forearms briskly and nervously. "Dawes was guarding Mrs. McCormick here until he supposedly went chasing after one of the civilians who was up to no good."

"Yes, sir, and evidently Dawes caught him. There were signs of a struggle, and Dawes's head had been caved in by several blows."

"Where was the body found?"

"A couple of hundred yards south of the town and the railroad tracks," replied Niland.

Claude must have moved the body, Faye thought, since the last time she had seen the corpse, it had been hidden in the shadows next to the cafe owner's adobe shack. She spoke up, saying, "That's the direction he was going when I saw him last."

"I'd say Sergeant Dawes was the first victim of the insurgents who later shot Private Hobart," Vickery decided. "At least, that's a reasonable explanation. You don't have anything else to add, do you, Mrs. McCormick?"

"I don't know anything about it," Faye declared. "I've already told you all I know."

"We'll see about that," Vickery said, and Faye didn't like the sound of his voice. He turned back to Niland and went on. "Clamp the lid down even tighter on the town, Major. I don't want any more trouble. Take those prisoners over to the jail and put them in the cells with Judge Schofield and Marshal Long." He smiled grimly. "We should be able to put on quite a convincing demonstration in the morning."

"You said you wouldn't kill anybody else!" Faye protested, her voice rising.

"I said no one would be harmed if everyone cooperated with us. Obviously, that hasn't been the case."

"You never intended to let anyone live!" Faye couldn't prevent the angry exclamation from slipping out. "You don't want to leave any witnesses behind! You're planning to murder the entire town!"

She could tell by the cold anger in Vickery's eyes that the accusations were true. Longarm had warned her about the same thing, and he had been right.

In his madness, Vickery was capable of *anything*.

For the moment, though, he was under control. He trained a baleful stare on Faye for a moment longer, then turned back to Niland. "Carry out your orders, Major. I'll deal with Mrs. McCormick."

Niland saluted and said, "Yes, sir." He turned and left the room.

Vickery faced Faye again and said, "I'm rather disappointed in you, Mrs. McCormick. I had hoped that you were starting to see me as I really am."

"I am," said Faye. "Oh, I certainly am."

The colonel flushed with anger once more. "Sacrifices are necessary in any military operation."

"So you're going to sacrifice an entire town just so you can hold a couple of politicians for ransom and embarrass the government?"

Vickery slammed a fist down on the side table, making Faye jump. "Damn it, woman, you don't understand! No one does! I have to show them, show them what a mistake they made!"

The army had made a mistake, all right, she thought. Vickery had been drummed out for incompetence, when he should have been locked up as a raving lunatic.

She didn't say that, not wanting to push him completely over the edge. Instead she took a deep breath and asked, "So what happens now?"

Her steady tone seemed to have a calming influence on him. "We wait until morning," Vickery said. He reached into his vest pocket and took out a large gold watch, which he opened to check the time. "It won't be long now, another couple of hours. Dawn comes fairly early around here in the summer, doesn't it?"

"The sun will be up by six o'clock," Faye replied grudgingly.

Vickery snapped the watch shut. "Excellent!"

His mood had improved dramatically again, Faye noted. Convinced that everything was once more under control, he had his mind on other things. As he came toward her, he continued, "You don't have to worry about yourself, of course, my dear. No harm will come to you. And *that* is a promise you can believe."

He was close to her now, within a foot of her. He lifted his hand and let his fingertips rest on her cheek as he stared down at her. She took another deep breath, forcing herself to remain calm, and said, "If you really cared for me, Colonel, you . . . you'd spare my friends."

"You won't need friends," he murmured. "You'll be coming with us when we leave this place."

That prospect filled Faye with horror, but she didn't allow the reaction to show on her face. "Where will we be going?" she asked.

"We have a camp across the border in Sonora. It's rather isolated, of course, but you'll be quite happy and comfortable there. All the comforts of home, as they say."

She doubted that. But if she got away from Vickery, it might help to know exactly where the gang's hideout was. "How do we get there? Tell me all about it."

"You don't need to know," he said, and for an instant she thought she had ventured too far, because his face hardened and his eyes grew more suspicious. The reaction was a brief one, though, and then he went on. "I'll take care of you. You don't have to worry about anything."

Vickery put a hand behind her head, holding her still as he leaned over to kiss her. This time Faye endured the kiss without struggling. She managed to do so by thinking about Custis Long. Had he escaped from the jail during the battle between Vickery's men and the townspeople recruited by Claude? That had been Longarm's plan, and if it had been successful, he might be coming for her soon. She held on to that hope, held on as tight as she possibly could.

Then guns began to crash and bang once more in the night.

Vickery tore his mouth away from hers. "Damn it!" he shouted. "What now?"

Releasing her, he turned once more to the window and looked out. When he straightened, his gun was in his hand.

"The shots are coming from the jail. That bastard Long must be trying to break out. I should have killed him before now." A vicious grin tugged at Vickery's mouth. "But if he's loose, he'll come here. He'll come for you, won't he, Mrs. McCormick? He won't run away and leave you in my hands. No, the noble Marshal Long, the famous Longarm, he couldn't do something like *that*!" Vickery lifted the gun in his hand and eared back the hammer. "And when he does come here . . . I'll be waiting. This time I'll put a bullet right in his brain."

Something snapped inside Faye at that moment. The strain of this violent, seemingly endless night was finally too much for her to stand. The threat to Longarm was the last straw. Faye threw herself across the room at Vickery and clawed at his face, seeking his eyes with her long fingernails. Somewhere outside the hotel, more guns were going off, and Faye vaguely heard the boom of what sounded like a shotgun.

The colonel roared in anger and backhanded her, savagely knocking her away from him. Faye tripped on the rug on the floor of the hotel room and fell, landing heavily on her left hip. Vickery came after her, looming over her. There were thin red streaks on his tanned features where her nails had ripped his skin.

"Slut!" he thundered. "I thought you were different! I thought you understood! But you're just like all the rest! You've been laughing at me, just like they laughed when I was forced to resign!"

Faye tried to slide away from him, but there was nowhere to go. She was lying next to the bed, and it hemmed her in on that side. Vickery had the other way blocked.

He swung the revolver in his hand toward her, and the muzzle of the gun looked as big around as a rain barrel. "There's only one thing to do now!" Vickery shouted as he lined the gun on her head.

Faye couldn't help it.

She screamed, loud and long.

Chapter 14

Longarm's head snapped up at the terrified shriek coming from the hotel. Beside him, Schofield reacted too, exclaiming, "My God! Was that Mrs. McCormick?"

"That's what I'm afraid of," Longarm said. He gave the judge a slight push toward the stable. "Get in there and saddle up three horses, if you can."

"What are you going to do?"

Longarm's face was grim as he replied, "Get Faye out of there—if I can." He hesitated, then added, "Once you've got the horses saddled up, get out of here. Don't wait for us."

"I understand," said Schofield. He broke the shotgun open, replaced the spent shells with a couple of fresh ones from his coat pocket, and trotted toward the barn, holding his injured left arm stiffly by his side.

Longarm went up the short, narrow flight of wooden steps to the back door of the hotel, knowing that within a matter of seconds more of Vickery's men would converge on this alley. Schofield would probably have to shoot his way out of the barn. Both Longarm and the judge were bucking heavy odds.

But this was the only game left.

The door opened before Longarm could reach it, and the outlaw who came to a sudden, stumbling stop on the threshold looked surprised as hell to see Longarm charging straight at him. The man tried to bring up the pistol in his hand, but Longarm was faster. The marshal slammed the butt of the Winchester into the outlaw's face, driving him backward. Blood spurted from the owlhoot's pulped nose. He fell onto his back like a sack of potatoes, already dead from the bone fragments that had sliced deep into his brain. Longarm hurdled over him and ran down the corridor, looking for a set of rear stairs.

He found one a few feet farther on and bounded up the steps, taking two and three with each leap. The Winchester was clutched tightly in his hands, ready for action. When he reached the top of the staircase, he grabbed the balustrade with one hand and hauled himself around sharply onto the landing. He could see the door to Vickery's room at the other end of the second-floor corridor. It was closed.

And since that first scream, there hadn't been another one.

His blood ice water in his veins, Longarm started down the hall toward the door.

"Very good," Vickery said, a twisted smile on his face. He lifted the gun so that it wasn't pointed right at Faye anymore. "If our friend Longarm is anywhere close by, that scream of yours will bring him running even faster, my dear."

Faye stared at him in horror. He hadn't intended to kill her after all. All he wanted was to draw Longarm to this hotel room. If the marshal thought she was in mortal danger, he would probably burst in here without taking the time to be careful.

And Vickery intended to be waiting for him.

Faye tried once more to get to her feet, but Vickery backhanded her with his free hand, the blow cracking across her face and sending her down to slump against the bed, half-senseless. He turned toward the door and moved over beside it, the revolver cocked and ready in his hand. As soon as Longarm came through the door, Vickery would be able to shoot him in the back.

Unless Faye somehow warned him . . .

Even in her stunned condition, she was able to understand that. She opened her mouth as footsteps pounded in the corridor outside, intending to call out to him and tell him to stay back. Before she could do so, something rammed against the door, which was unlocked.

That something was Longarm's shoulder, and under the force of the collision, the door sprang open. Longarm half-ran, half-stumbled into the room.

Faye surged to her feet, a warning cry seemingly frozen on her lips, and lunged forward as Vickery brought his gun down to line his sights on Longarm. The colonel's hand seemed to be barely moving as Faye threw herself across the room. She crashed into a startled Longarm as smoke and flame belched from the muzzle of Vickery's gun. The two of them fell as the bullet whined through the space where the back of Longarm's head had been only an instant earlier.

Longarm landed on his shoulder and rolled toward Vickery. Faye saw what was happening from where she was sprawled on the floor. The colonel tried to jerk his pistol down for another shot at Longarm, but before he could bring it to bear, Longarm thrust the Winchester up one-handed and rammed the barrel into Vickery's belly. Vickery gasped in pain and doubled over.

Longarm came up on one knee and slapped the stock of the rifle against the side of Vickery's head, knocking the colonel off his feet. At the same instant, shouts came from the hallway. Faye heard Major Niland barking, ''Don't shoot! You might hit the colonel! Get in there and grab Long!''

Faye and Longarm scrambled to their feet at the same moment. Longarm grabbed Faye's hand and tugged her toward one of the windows. ''Come on!'' he said.

She went, having a pretty good idea what he intended but not sure she could do it. Vickery was still writhing on the floor in pain as Faye and Longarm reached the window. He used the barrel of the Winchester to smash the glass and rake out the larger pieces. A gun went off from the doorway and the bullet chewed splinters from the frame of the window not far from Longarm's head. He winced as some of the splinters stung his cheek.

He turned and fired the Winchester one-handed toward the door while helping Faye through the window with the other hand. She saw the awning that ran along the front of the hotel only a few feet below her, and her heart seemed to stop as she let go of Longarm's hand and let herself fall. He plunged out of the window right behind her.

They hit the awning, which held for a second and broke their fall before it tore and dumped them the rest of the way to the ground. Pain shot through Faye's right leg as she landed, but when Longarm grabbed her arm and hauled her to her feet, she was able to stand up without the leg buckling under her. Longarm looked around, obviously trying to decide which way to run—and which direction the next threat would come from.

Hooves suddenly pounded in the darkness, seemingly right on top of her. Faye's head jerked around, and she gave a choked cry as she saw the horses looming up out of the night practically right on top of her, just about to run her down.

Longarm reached for Faye, intending to try to throw her out of the way of the plunging horses, even if he got trampled in the process. But then he saw the thickset figure in the saddle of one of the mounts and heard the man yelling, "Whoa! Whoa, damn it!" at the horses. The rider had all three sets of reins in one pudgy hand, and he hauled back on them with all of his strength. Rearing up on their hind legs, the horses skidded to a stop. In doing so, they raised a thick, choking cloud of dust.

Longarm was thankful for that. Under the circumstances, any cover was better than none. He took hold of Faye's arm and nearly threw her into one of the empty saddles. "Hang on!" he called to her.

Gunmen tumbled from the front door of the hotel. Longarm sent four shots screaming among them, firing as fast as he could work the lever of the Winchester. The outlaws scattered, returning the fire. Longarm hoped none of the bullets struck any of the horses.

He grabbed the saddlehorn on the third riderless horse and swung up, not even waiting until his rear end hit the leather before kicking the horse into a run. It nearly lunged out from underneath him as it broke into a gallop, but he clamped his thighs on the animal's flanks and managed to stay on. Schofield and Faye were right in front of him, both of them riding awkwardly but hanging on for dear life as their mounts raced along Inferno's only street toward the east.

Longarm leaned forward over the neck of his horse to make himself a smaller target. As he drew up alongside Schofield, he called over to the judge, "I told you to get out of town and not worry about us!"

"I thought about it!" Schofield shouted back. "Believe me, I thought about it! But it seemed the shortest way out of town was around the front of the hotel!"

That wasn't true, and both of them knew it. Schofield must have a few reserves of decency left in him after all, Longarm thought. But they could talk about that later, after the threat of Vickery had been dealt with.

The hurricane deck of a running horse was no place for accurate shooting, but as fireflies of orange muzzle fire winked at them from the darkness, Longarm flung a few wild return shots at the flashes. Then they were past the tiny railroad station and the water tank on its stilt-like legs, and Inferno fell behind them. Bullets thudded into the ground behind them, while other slugs screamed past overhead, but none of the outlaw lead touched the riders or their mounts.

There was a fierce grin on Longarm's face as he looked back at the settlement. He was certain that Vickery would send some men after them; the colonel couldn't afford to let them escape without at least trying to recapture them. But by the time any pursuit could be mounted, he and Faye and Schofield would have a small lead, and in the darkness, that might be enough. The moon hadn't set yet, but it was low down in the western sky and provided only a feeble reddish glow, unlike the brighter silvery light that had

131

washed over the arid landscape earlier in the night.

What he really wanted to do, once he and his companions had put some space between themselves and Inferno, was find a place to call a short halt so that they could figure out their next move. It was probably too late to reach the next railroad stop to the east before the train got there, but that didn't matter. Longarm might be able to stop that westbound train from rolling into Inferno in a couple of hours. He could build a fire on the tracks if he had to, in order to stop the locomotive and warn them of the robbery Vickery had planned.

But once he realized his scheme had been ruined, Vickery would cut and run, and he might leave the town in flames behind him. Longarm wanted to stop that if he could. After everything that Vickery had done, Longarm wanted to bring the colonel to justice.

And failing that, putting a bullet through the son of a bitch's head might serve just as well.

"He's going to *what*?"

Longarm's voice was filled with amazement as he looked at Faye in the faint light of the moon and stars. She had just told him what Vickery had revealed to her about Vice President Wheeler and the Mexican diplomat, and although Longarm found the story difficult to believe, he wouldn't really put such a bold scheme beyond Vickery. The really bad part about it was that the renegade ex-colonel might just carry it off.

Longarm, Faye, and Schofield were in a dry wash a couple of miles from Inferno, underneath the trestle on which the tracks of the Southern Pacific crossed the gully. Confident that they had given the slip to the men who had followed them out of the settlement, Longarm thought it was safe enough to stop briefly and let their horses rest. That had given Faye a chance to assure him that she was all right and to repeat the amazing things Vickery had told her in that hotel room.

"Can he do it?" asked Schofield as he stood holding the reins of his horse. "Does he actually think he can kidnap the Vice President of the United States and get away with it?''

"I don't know," Longarm said dryly. "Do you think a local judge could get away with sentencing a U.S. marshal to slave labor in a Mexican silver mine on some trumped-up charges?''

Schofield *harummphed* in embarrassment. "I was perhaps a bit too hasty," he began. "Under the circumstances—''

"Under the circumstances, I won't say anything else about it," Longarm said, "but don't think I've forgotten, Judge." He paused. "I won't forget about the way you came around the hotel with these horses either.''

Schofield squared his shoulders, grunting in pain from his wounded arm. "Right now I suggest we concentrate on deciding what to do about that madman who still has Inferno in his grip.''

Longarm nodded. "Yep. I figure the first thing to do is stop that train so that Vickery doesn't have a chance to snatch the Vice President.''

"What about the Mexican representative?'' asked Faye.

"There's not much we can do about him," Longarm replied with a shrug of his broad shoulders. "We don't know exactly what trail he'll be taking into town, nor when he'll arrive. But we do know the train the Vice President is on can't get into Inferno except on those tracks." He pointed to the trestle above their heads. "And in answer to your question, Judge, I think Vickery *can* kidnap that old son from Washington—unless we stop him. We killed a few of his boys back there, but he's still got plenty of guns. If he takes the Vice President's escort by surprise . . .'' Longarm shrugged again. "I reckon he can do just about anything he wants.''

Schofield tugged on his grizzled beard. "All right. We'll stop the train. It's too late to do anything else.''

"You and Faye can handle that part of it," Longarm said. "I had something else in mind.''

Faye looked at him in alarm. "Oh, Custis, you're not going back there, are you?''

"There's a score to settle with Vickery," Longarm replied grimly. "Not to mention the fact that he's an outlaw and I'm a duly sworn lawman. I can't just ignore what he's done.''

''You can let somebody else catch him!''

''You said yourself he's got a hideout somewhere over the border in Mexico, and he can reach the border mighty damn quick from Inferno. The only real chance we've got of catching him is to get him while he's waiting for the train to roll in.''

''One man against twenty or thirty bloodthirsty owlhoots?'' Judge Schofield asked in astonishment. ''That's suicide, Long!''

''Maybe not. If I can slip back into town and get my hands on Vickery, the others are liable to light a shuck when they realize the train's not coming. Vickery's made 'em put up that military facade, but at heart they're still a gang of outlaws, looking out for themselves first. I don't think any loyalty to Vickery will hold them for very long, especially once they figure out the cavalry's liable to be on their trail mighty soon.''

''Well . . . you may be right,'' Schofield said, still doubtful.

''It's still too dangerous,'' Faye declared.

Longarm reached out and cupped her chin. ''Sorry, Faye,'' he said softly, ''but this is just something I've got to do.''

''Oh . . . oh . . . shoot!'' She moved against him and rested her head on his chest. ''I know you do, Custis. I just wish there was some other way.'' She looked up at him. ''I could go back with you—''

''Not hardly,'' he said firmly, ''not after that time we had getting you out of there.''

Schofield spoke up. ''We're all mighty lucky not to be dead.''

Longarm had to agree with that. He said, ''How about giving us a minute, Judge.''

''Oh. Oh, yes, of course,'' said Schofield. ''I'll just go up to the top of this wash and take a look around, make sure Vickery's men aren't about to stumble over us.''

''That sounds like a good idea.''

When the judge had clambered up the steep bank of the wash, leaving Longarm and Faye in the shadows underneath the trestle, Longarm tightened his arms around her and brought his mouth down on hers. Faye responded eagerly, hungrily, and there was more than a hint of desperation in her kiss. After a long moment, she drew away from him and whispered, "Don't you dare go back there and get yourself killed, Custis Long. Even if it means letting Vickery get away."

"I don't intend to get killed . . . or to let that son of a bitch get away."

"Custis . . . when this is all over . . ." She broke off and gave a little shake of her head. "No, I'm not going to do it. I'm not going to talk about the future. It's all too uncertain."

"Life generally is," Longarm told her, and then he kissed her again. They had the here and now, and that was what counted.

Chapter 15

Claude sat on the bunk in the jail cell and tried not to groan in pain. His right leg throbbed miserably where a bullet had burned across the outside of his thigh. Still, he was lucky to be alive to hurt, he told himself. That was more than Dutch and old Ab Peeler could say. They were both dead, cut down by Vickery's gunmen, far beyond feeling anything.

The eight prisoners in the jail cell were mostly older men; only one, in fact, was below the age of forty. They had fought battles and endured hardships in the past. They had taken up arms in the Civil War, and most of them before that in the Mexican War. They had fought Apaches and the elements to carve out lives for themselves in Arizona Territory. Claude counted all of them as his friends. He had gone to them with Faye's plea for help, and they had responded. And what had they accomplished?

Two good men were dead, and the rest of them were locked up awaiting execution.

Claude hoped it had been worth it.

The cell block door opened, and that bearded outlaw, the one called Niland, stalked in. "On your feet," he snapped at the prisoners.

"What for?" asked Claude.

"The colonel wants to talk to you."

137

Claude snorted. "He can do that just as good with me sittin' on my ass."

Niland's features clenched angrily, but Vickery came into the cell block behind him and said, "It's all right, Major. I'm accustomed to disrespect from the likes of them." He faced the cell where the eight men were locked up. "Actually, I rather admire you men. You showed some courage, at least, instead of simply capitulating like everyone else in town."

"If that two-bit word means givin' up, it ain't in our natures," Claude said defiantly.

"Nor is it in mine," replied Vickery. "I just thought you'd like to know that your ploy was unsuccessful. Your little distraction didn't work. Judge Schofield and Marshal Long are both dead. They were killed trying to escape from the jail."

Claude's breath stuck in his throat for a moment; then he was able to ask, "What about Faye?"

Vickery smiled. "The lovely Mrs. McCormick is in my hotel room at this moment, waiting for me. She'll be accompanying us when we leave Inferno in about . . ." He pulled a watch from his pocket and checked the time. "About an hour and a half from now."

Claude came to his feet, wincing as his weight came down on his wounded leg. "Damn you, Vickery!" he exclaimed. "You got no right to haul that gal off. She never did anything to hurt you."

Vickery smiled thinly and said, "My rights are what I make of them, old man. And I claim the right to take what I want and kill anyone who gets in my way."

"Sounds like owlhoot talk to me," Claude snapped recklessly. "I thought you was supposed to be some sort of soldier."

Vickery's shoulders lifted and fell in a little shrug. "Some dreams have to be put aside in exchange for others." He looked over at Niland. "Maintain the guard on these men, Major. My earlier orders still stand. We'll deal with them after our other business is concluded."

Deal with them, Claude thought to himself. That meant kill them. Vickery intended to have all eight of them shot whenever he was finished with whatever hellish plan had brought him to Inferno in the first place. Claude was sure of it.

Vickery turned on his heels and marched out of the cell block, followed by Major Niland. Claude sank down on the bunk again and sighed, trying not to give in to bitter despair.

The judge and that fella called Longarm were both dead, Vickery had said, and Faye was a prisoner too. Some folks would say she was facing an even worse fate than Claude and his companions.

The worst part of it was that Vickery would probably have them shot down like dogs. It would have been better if he could have gone down fighting, Claude thought, a gun in his hands, killing those sons of bitches who had ridden in and taken over the town. . . .

Maybe when the guards took them out, he could jump one of the bastards and get his hands on a gun. He could do more than a little damage before they shot him to ribbons. Claude looked down at his gnarled old hand and could almost feel the fingers curling around the smooth walnut grips of a smokepole. . . .

It was something to think on, while he waited for his last night on earth to be over.

Longarm left the horse about a quarter of a mile south of Inferno, tying its reins loosely to a scrubby mesquite tree so that it could eventually pull loose and instinctively trot back to where it had come from, the livery barn behind the hotel. He wasn't going to be needing a mount again tonight.

If things didn't work out right, he probably wouldn't ever need a horse again, unless they had owlhoots to chase in the hereafter.

He put that grim thought out of his head and started cat-footing toward the lights of the settlement, staying low to take advantage of what skimpy cover there was. Mesquites, a few large rocks, and an occasional gully in which he could get down and crawl along on hands and knees provided a little concealment, and Longarm intended to use all of it he could.

He had no watch, but to a veteran frontiersman, the sky was enough of a clock. To the east, the heavens had taken on a grayish tinge. Soon that would lighten to a red glow as dawn approached, shading through orange and gold until the fiery orb itself peeked over the horizon. That time was perhaps than an hour away, Longarm judged, no more than that.

Maybe that train was running a mite behind schedule. That would come in handy if it was true. But it was pretty unlikely, what with the Vice President on board, bound for a secret, high-level meeting. Everyone involved with the railroad, from the president of the Southern Pacific on down to the lowliest porters, would be trying to make sure the train arrived when it was supposed to.

Longarm had reloaded both of his pistols with cartridges from the shell belt he wore. He didn't have any spare cartridges for the Winchester, but there were still eight bullets in the rifle. He had used the lever to eject them, then counted them and fed them back into the Winchester's magazine. That wasn't enough ammunition to fight a pitched battle, but he thought it would be sufficient for his purposes.

If one of those bullets wound up in Vickery's brain, Longarm didn't really care about the rest.

When he was within a hundred yards of the town, he became even more cautious. After everything that had happened tonight, Vickery was probably pretty spooked. Doubtless he had posted extra guards. But he didn't have enough men to put a sentry in front and back of every building in town, as he might have liked. There had to be at least one unguarded approach.

Longarm flattened himself on the ground and studied what he could see of Inferno for several minutes. The settlement appeared to be quiet, and if not for all the lights burning, a person might have thought that everybody in town was asleep.

The sudden thudding of hoofbeats nearby made Longarm stiffen. Beads of cold sweat popped out on his forehead. He turned his head, being careful not to move too quickly, and spotted several men on horseback about twenty yards to his left. They weren't coming directly at him, but if they continued on their current path, they would pass pretty close to him. He looked around, saw a dark line a few feet to his right, and slithered in that direction.

The darkness on the ground was a little brush-choked coulee, just as he had hoped it would be. He slid into the concealment of the hardy desert bushes and held his breath. Those riders had to be some of Vickery's men, and they were probably searching for him. Longarm couldn't think of any other reason for anybody to be abroad so early in the morning.

A voice floated to his ears over the sound of the horses. "—not looking forward to it, I tell you," the man was saying.

"Me neither," agreed another man. "But I reckon we got to report anyway. The colonel wouldn't have it otherwise."

"I wish we were bringing back that bastard's head instead of reporting that him and the others got away. *That* would make the colonel happy, if we could toss it at his feet and he could see that damned marshal looking up at him."

Oh, yeah, thought Longarm. *They are Vickery's men, all right.*

A third man spoke up. Longarm couldn't catch all the words, because the riders had passed him by now and were moving out of earshot, but he heard," . . . bloodthirsty son of a bitch . . . execute those prisoners . . ."

They had to be talking about the bunch Claude had gotten together to stage that distraction. Longarm hoped the old cafe owner was still alive; he had promised Faye he would try to find out what had happened to Claude.

There was only one place where Vickery was liable to be holding the survivors of the attempted uprising, and that was in the late Sheriff Carl Thurgood's jail. Longarm didn't relish going back there, since he had spent so much of the past twenty or so hours there and had already broken out of the place twice, but he thought it was unlikely there would be guards around in back. The jail was so solidly built that the only real way in was through the front. That was where the outlaws would be.

Longarm wanted to talk to the prisoners and find out how much they knew about what had gone on in the settlement since he and Faye and Schofield had ridden out. Besides, if he could somehow manage to free the captives, they would make good allies in the inevitable fight. He was able to pick out the big stone building where the jail was located, and since the riders were out of sight, he deemed it safe to slide out of the coulee and start crawling toward town again.

Major Niland took a deep breath and said, "Far be it from me to question your judgment, Colonel—"

"Then don't," snapped Vickery.

Niland plunged ahead. "But are you certain we shouldn't call off the mission? If Long and the others warn the military escort on the Vice President's train—"

Vickery interrupted again. "They won't. The nearest town to the east of here is at least a four-hour ride away. The train will be here long before the marshal and his companions can reach the authorities."

"What if they stop the train itself?"

Vickery shook his head confidently. "The train won't stop for them. Think about it, Major. The engineer of that train knows that he's carrying the Vice President of the United States. He's not going to stop for a couple of armed men who, for all he knows, intend to rob the train or even threaten the Vice President." Vickery took one of his cigars from his vest pocket, rolled it between his fingers, smelled it, and put it in his mouth. Around the tightly wrapped cylinder of tobacco, he said, "No, Major, as disappointed as I am that Long and Schofield and Mrs. McCormick escaped, I know it's much too late for them to endanger our mission. In an hour, perhaps even less, we will be one step closer to more wealth than you've ever dreamed of. And I will have struck back against the ungrateful government that turned me out."

"Yes, sir," Niland said. "You're right, of course."

But despite that, he would feel a lot better when they were back across the border with the Vice President and that Mexican representative, waiting for the fortune in ransom they would demand. It was a bold, audacious plan, daring almost to the point of lunacy.

That was appropriate, thought Niland, since Colonel Vickery himself was a raving lunatic. As with many madmen, however, there was a spark of genius in the colonel. He had come up with this scheme that was going to make all of them very rich men. That was all Niland cared about. The big payoff would be worth all the military bullshit Vickery forced them to endure.

Niland's fingertips lightly brushed the butt of his gun. And when it was all over, he mused, when they had the money and they didn't need the colonel anymore . . .

Major Niland didn't finish the thought, but it was still enough to make him smile.

Faye and Judge Schofield followed the rails of the Southern Pacific, heading east, and from time to time the judge called a halt, dismounted, and bent over to feel of the steel ribbon. After about the sixth stop, he looked up excitedly at Faye. "I can feel vibrations in the rail," he said. "The train's coming."

She lifted herself in the saddle and peered along the rail line, hoping to see the headlight of the onrushing locomotive. After a moment she pointed and cried, "There it is!"

The light was small and distant, but it grew rapidly. Schofield said, "Let's get these horses away from the tracks."

They led the animals about fifty yards away and tied the reins to one of the scrubby little bushes that dotted the sandy landscape. Schofield pulled up a couple of the smaller bushes. Then they hurried back to the tracks.

"I think those scoundrels left me a match or two," Schofield muttered as he searched in the pockets of his coat. "Ah, yes, there they are! Hold these, my dear." He handed her the bushes.

Faye held them well away from her body as Schofield scratched one of the matches into life and held the flame to the dried leaves clinging to the bushes. The leaves were stubborn, but after a moment they caught and began to burn brightly.

By now the train was close enough so that both of them could hear the rumble of the engine. Schofield took the makeshift torch from Faye and stepped closer to the tracks, waving the burning bushes back and forth as he did so. The noise grew louder and louder, and Faye waited impatiently for the sound of the engineer applying the brakes.

The sound didn't come. Surely the train's crew there in the engine's cab had seen Schofield signaling with the blazing bushes. Why weren't they stopping?

Suddenly, Faye stepped up beside Schofield and gripped his free arm. "Judge," she said anxiously, "what if they think we're outlaws? Maybe they won't stop for us!"

"Dear Lord, you're right!" exclaimed Schofield. "I didn't think of that." He began waving the torch more frantically.

The headlight of the locomotive was like the huge, smoldering eye of a great beast lumbering toward them. The train wasn't slowing down at all. In fact, it seemed to have increased its speed, as if the engineer was pouring more steam to the drivers. Faye realized abruptly that she and Schofield were standing practically on top of the rails. She tugged at his arm and said, "Come on, Judge, we have to get out of the way!"

"They're not stopping!" thundered Schofield. "By God, why aren't they stopping?"

The light washed over them, throwing its harsh glare in their faces. Faye jerked Schofield backward with all of her strength as the locomotive loomed up and roared past them. The wind of the speeding train's passage sucked violently at them and threatened to pull them underneath the wheels. Both Faye and Schofield stumbled backward until they fell. The blazing bushes hit the ground when Schofield dropped them, but the flames continued to burn brightly for several moments before they went out.

All Faye could do was lie there and looked up in dismay at the train rolling past them. Somewhere in there, she thought, was the Vice President of the United States, and unknown to that high official and the men guarding him, disaster waited a few miles down the tracks. Unless Longarm had somehow been able to put a stop to Colonel Vickery's plan, the Vice President would soon be in the hands of as vicious a pack of outlaws as he was ever likely to encounter.

Yes, thought Faye as tears of frustration rolled down her cheeks, it was all up to Longarm now.

Chapter 16

Claude thought he was hearing things at first. But sure enough, somebody was really calling his name in a low voice that was little more than a whisper. He lifted his head and looked around with a frown, then realized the summons was coming from the narrow, barred window on the other side of the cell.

The other men in the cell had all dozed off, exhaustion claiming them despite their perilous situation. Claude was the only one still awake. He stood up from the bunk and crossed the cell, reaching up to grasp the bars in the window. "Who's out there?" he hissed.

"It's Marshal Long," came the reply.

Claude's eyes widened in surprise. "Long!" he repeated. "But you're dead!"

There was a chuckle in the deep darkness behind the jail. "Not so's you notice," said Longarm.

Leaning closer to the bars, Claude asked anxiously, "What about Faye? And Judge Schofield?"

"Both of them were all right when I left them. The judge's arm got ventilated by a bullet, but the wound seemed pretty clean. I tied it up when we stopped for a breather after getting out of town and away from Vickery's men."

"That son of a bitch told us you and the judge was dead and said he had Faye locked up in his hotel room," whispered Claude. "That lyin' bastard!"

"Take it easy," Longarm advised him. "Faye and the judge have gone to stop the westbound before it ever gets here, and I came back for Vickery."

"You can't take him by yourself. Hell, it'd be crazy to try!"

Longarm laughed again. "Nobody's ever accused me of being overly sane. Here, take this." He passed something through the bars.

Claude reached up and took the gun. It was a Colt .45, and it felt damned good in his hand.

"Hide that under your shirt," Longarm told him. "I may get a chance to bust you out of there, but even if I don't, you're liable to need a gun before all this is over."

"You're askin' for our help again? Last time we tried that, two good men wound up dead." Claude's naturally contrary nature asserted itself as he asked, "Why should we chance something like that again?"

"I'm not asking you to fight for me," Longarm said. "I'm asking you to fight for yourselves. I would've thought an old-timer like you would be used to handling your own trouble."

Claude frowned and muttered, "Yeah, I reckon you're right. What're you goin' to do, Long?"

"Try to get my hands on Vickery some way. I figure once I do, the others won't give as much trouble. When they find out that train's not coming, they're liable to cut and run."

Claude nodded in agreement and tucked the pistol behind his belt, pulling out his shirt so that the tail hung down over the Colt's grip. "All right. If you can get me out of here, I'll give you a hand. If not . . . well, give 'em hell, Long."

"I intend to," promised Longarm. "I sure intend to."

Longarm moved away from the rear of the jail in a crouch, the Winchester in one hand, the remaining revolver in the other. He stuck to the darkest shadows and kept his eyes constantly searching. A couple of buildings away, he spotted a tiny pinprick of orange which might have been the glowing tip of a cigarette. Vickery wouldn't like it if he knew his men were smoking on guard duty. Longarm was mighty grateful for it, though.

Like an Apache, he slipped silently through the darkness, well aware that the sky to the east had grown lighter still. Soon, it would be too light for him to move around the settlement as easily. If he was going to accomplish what he had come here for, he would have to do it without wasting much more time.

The building where the guard was posted was a store of some sort; Longarm wasn't familiar enough with Inferno to remember what was sold there. But the rear of the building had a high porch built on it, so that freight wagons could back up there and unload directly onto the porch. Longarm reached the end of it and ducked down, sliding underneath the thick planks that sat on support beams.

The darkness under the porch was so thick it was almost solid. Longarm edged through it in an uncomfortable crouch, hoping fervently there weren't any rattlers coiled up on the sand around him. This was just the sort of hiding place they would like. He heard the boards creak over his head as the guard moved a little, and he was able to use the sound to guide him. A moment later, he reached a spot under the edge of the porch that was directly under the outlaw.

Longarm leaned over and noiselessly placed the Winchester on the sand at his feet. Then he reached up with his free hand and scratched on the underside of the porch, just loud enough to be heard a few feet away. He heard a muttered "Huh?" and the guard's cigarette arched out away from the porch to land on the hard-packed dirt of the rear alley. Longarm scratched again.

Above him, the guard leaned out from the edge of the porch and bent over in an attempt to peer underneath it. He probably thought there was some sort of animal under here, but he would have to check that out to be certain. A match flared in his hand.

At the same instant, Longarm came out from under the porch and uncoiled lithely from his crouch. He thrust the barrel of the Winchester up, driving it into the solar plexus of the guard. The man grunted as the wind was knocked out

149

of him, and he couldn't catch his breath to cry out. Longarm reached up and grabbed his belt buckle, hauling him off the porch.

The guard sprawled onto the ground and clawed at his holstered gun. Longarm lifted the rifle and brought it down in a smooth, deadly stroke. The brass-plated butt of the Winchester's stock struck the guard's head with a dull thud, crushing his skull. The outlaw gurgled and died.

That was one more he wouldn't have to deal with, Longarm thought grimly. He took the man's pistol and shoved it behind his belt.

Then, thinking quickly, he picked up the guard's hat as well, which had fallen off when Longarm jerked the man off the porch. It was just like the Stetsons worn by the other members of the gang, neatly creased and brushed free of dust. Longarm settled it on his head, then pulled the man's coat off as well. The plan he had in mind was risky, but it might be his best chance of getting close enough to Vickery to grab the renegade colonel.

The dead man's coat was a mite short in the sleeves, and Longarm didn't figure he could button it across his chest, but the fit was close enough to be passable. He glanced at the eastern sky again. Half an hour until sunrise, he judged.

Then, taking a deep breath, he walked up the alley next to the building and stepped out onto Inferno's only street.

The hotel, he saw, was three doors to his right. He turned in that direction, keeping his head down as he walked. His skin crawled as he passed one of the outlaws, who called softly to him, "Hey, Harley, where're you goin'?"

Longarm gestured toward the hotel without looking up. Making his voice as guttural as possible, he said, "Colonel wants to see me."

The other man chuckled. "Glad it's you and not me who's goin' to get his ass chewed."

Longarm grunted, but didn't say anything else. The man appeared satisfied that he was the owlhoot called Harley. If he could get by the others that easily, he might just have a chance of pulling this off.

Of course, it was unlikely that it would be that simple. For one thing, he would probably run into Major Niland before he reached Vickery, and the bearded outlaw wouldn't be fooled by Longarm's crude masquerade. Longarm would probably have to shoot his way past Niland.

Which he was more than willing to do, if it came down to that.

Longarm didn't encounter any more outlaws before he reached the front doors of the hotel. He grasped the knob of one of the doors, turned it, and stepped inside, lifting his head just enough for a quick glance around the lobby before he dropped his eyes toward the floor again. There were two gunmen lounging in chairs near the desk, but other than that the lobby was deserted. Any guests unlucky enough to be staying in the place when Vickery took over would be lying low in their rooms, more than likely. There was no sign of the nervous-looking clerk. He had probably been locked up in a storeroom or some such, thought Longarm.

One of the outlaws looked up from his chair. "What do you want?" he asked in a surly voice. Obviously, the military discipline enforced by Vickery and Niland was lacking when neither of the two boss owlhoots were around.

"Colonel wanted to see me," Longarm said as he jerked his head toward the stairs beyond the desk.

"Nobody said anything to us about that," said the second man. "We ain't supposed to let anybody up there without orders."

Longarm shrugged and started to turn back toward the entrance. "Fine by me. I didn't particularly want to see the colonel anyway. Wonder what he wanted."

"Hang on, damn it," said one of the guards as he scraped his chair back and stood up. "I don't want to get crosswise with the colonel. Go on up, and if you're wrong, it'll be on your head."

"Yeah, yeah," muttered Longarm. He brushed past the man and started up the stairs.

"Hold on, Quint," the second man said abruptly. "Look at that fella's boots!"

151

As soon as Longarm heard the tone of alarm in the outlaw's voice, he knew his daring gamble was over. Instinctively, he glanced down at his boots and saw how dusty and scratched up they were, unlike the polished boots of the outlaws.

Still, he tried to brazen it out. "Yeah, they look pretty bad, don't they? I've got to shine 'em up as soon as I get the chance. I sure hate to go see the colonel looking like this."

For a second, he thought his bluff was going to pay off. The first man grunted and started to turn back toward his chair, but the second one grabbed his arm. "Something's wrong!" he snapped. "That's Harley's coat, but that sure as hell ain't Harley!"

"By God, you're right!" exclaimed the outlaw called Quint. He reached for his gun as he ordered Longarm, "Wait just a damned minute—"

Longarm wasn't waiting for anything. Quint was still within reach of Longarm's leg, so he lashed out with his foot and drove the heel of his boot into the outlaw's jaw. Quint went flying backward, arms flying.

At the same time, Longarm palmed out the Colt on his hip. He hadn't wanted to start the ball quite so soon; it would have been better if he had been closer to Vickery before any shots broke out. But the second guard was already clawing his revolver from leather, so Longarm couldn't wait. The gun in his hand bucked against his palm as he aimed at the tag hanging from the sack of tobacco in the man's shirt pocket. The outlaw was thrown backward by the slug boring into his chest.

Longarm whirled, confident that the man he had kicked in the head would be out of the fight for a while. He bounded up the stairs, lunging for the second-floor landing. When he reached it, he turned toward the front of the hotel and headed for Vickery's room.

Niland must have been in there with the colonel, because he came out of the room with a gun in his hand, looking for the source of the shot. The fact that the man charging toward him was wearing the hat and coat of one of the outlaws must have confused him for a second, because he hesitated just long enough to allow Longarm to get in the first shot. Flame licked from the muzzle of the gun in the lawman's hand as Longarm fired.

The bullet clipped Niland on top of the left shoulder and threw him back as if a giant hand had just slapped him. Niland cried out in pain, but he managed to catch his balance and still had his gun in his right hand. The weapon boomed, sending a slug screaming past Longarm's ear.

Then Longarm crashed into the major, driving him back again. The open door of Vickery's room was right behind him, and both men tumbled through it. Longarm slapped the barrel of the pistol against the side of Niland's head as they sprawled on the floor, and he felt the outlaw go limp underneath him.

Longarm was trying to scramble to his feet when something slammed into his side and sent him rolling. "Long!" a furious voice roared. Colonel Vickery came after him, leg drawn back for another brutal kick.

Reaching up, Longarm grabbed Vickery's boot and heaved with all his strength, sending the colonel sailing backward. Pain shot through Longarm's torso, and he wondered if Vickery's first kick had broken some of his ribs when it landed.

There was no time to worry about that now. Somehow, Longarm had managed to hang on to the revolver, although the Winchester had slipped from his fingers and gone clattering to the floor of the hotel room. He came up on his knees and pivoted at the waist, turning toward the door as another of the outlaws appeared there, gun in hand. Longarm's pistol boomed, and the man doubled over with a scream as he caught lead in the stomach. He dropped his gun and pitched onto his face.

Longarm swung back toward Vickery, who was just regaining his feet. "Freeze, Colonel!" Longarm ordered as he lined the sights of the Colt on the outlaw leader.

Vickery stood motionless except for his chest, which was heaving with emotion as he glared at Longarm. "My God, Long," he said, "what are you doing back here?"

"Figured you and I had some unfinished business," Longarm grated. He heard rapid footsteps on the stairs from the lobby. "You'd best call off your dogs, or I'll finish it right here and now and take my chances with the rest of your bunch."

"You'll never get out of here alive!"

"Neither will you," Longarm said coolly.

Vickery hesitated, and Longarm wasn't sure what the colonel was going to do next. He didn't get a chance to find out, because Niland came up off the floor and grabbed the wrist of Longarm's gun hand, jerking it down. At the same time the major hooked a punch into Longarm's midsection.

Longarm hadn't expected Niland to regain his senses quite so quickly. In fact, Niland was fighting primarily on instinct, Longarm realized. The major's expression was still pretty fuzzy. But his quick action had turned the tide, and while Longarm was forced to grapple with Niland, Vickery pulled his gun and lunged forward.

Longarm felt the barrel of the revolver digging painfully into the back of his head. He winced and froze, and Vickery said, "If you move again, Marshal, I shall take great pleasure in blowing your brains out."

"Do it, Colonel!" panted Niland. "Kill the son of a bitch!"

More men poured into the room, and hands grabbed Longarm's shoulders and arms. He was jerked to his feet as Vickery took the gun away from his head and plucked the pistol from his hand. "Not just yet," said the colonel. "I want Marshal Long to live a while longer. I want to see the expression on his face when we kidnap the Vice President of the United States."

Longarm looked through slitted eyes at Vickery. "If you expect me to be all shocked by what you just said, old son, you're going to be disappointed. I know all about it. Mrs. McCormick told me everything you let on to her."

Vickery shrugged. "I thought that might be the case. It doesn't really matter."

"Maybe not, but you got another disappointment coming. The judge has stopped that train by now. There's not going to be any kidnapping."

No sooner were the words out of Longarm's mouth, however, than a sound drifted in through the open window of the hotel room, a sound that chilled Longarm's blood as it cut through the still air of impending dawn.

It was the whistle of a train, approaching Inferno.

Chapter 17

A sardonic smile stretched across Vickery's lean face. "It appears that you're incorrect, Marshal," he said. "Unless I'm sadly mistaken, that's the westbound about to pull in right now."

Longarm tried not to let his spirits sink, but it was hard to stay optimistic under the circumstances. He had gone and gotten himself captured again, and obviously Faye and Schofield had failed to stop the train.

"Quickly now," snapped Vickery to his men. "I want everyone in position when the train comes to a stop beside the water tank. Major, are you all right?"

"I'm fine now, Colonel," replied Niland. With the hand that wasn't holding a gun trained on Longarm, he touched the lump that was rising on his head above his ear. "My head's still ringing a little, but it won't stop me from gunning down this son of a bitch."

"Don't kill him yet," said Vickery. "I want him to see this. You're in charge of the prisoner, Major."

"Yes, sir." Niland stepped up to Longarm and prodded him viciously with the barrel of his gun. "Get moving."

Longarm had no choice but to do as he was told. He left the hotel room and went downstairs, followed by Vickery and Niland. The other outlaws who had come running when the fight broke out had already headed for the train station.

As Longarm emerged from the hotel into the street, he saw several members of the gang scurrying here and there, getting ready to ambush the soldiers escorting the Vice President. In the shadowy half-light, they were like phantoms.

"Keep going," Niland ordered. "Keep your hands down. We don't want anybody on that train to see you as it's pulling in and get the idea that something's wrong."

Longarm was seething inside. It seemed impossible that he could have gone through everything he had endured during the past day, only to fail here at the last minute in his bid to stop Vickery's plan. Not only that, but he had not had a chance to free Claude and the other prisoners from the jail, and it was clear that Vickery intended to execute them. Hell, that madman might kill everybody in the whole town before he was finished. And as far as Longarm could see right now, there was no way in hell to save himself or anybody else—including Vice President Wheeler.

As the group reached the tiny station building, Longarm looked around. Several gunmen were concealed behind the station, while others had scattered along the tracks and hidden themselves behind rocks and mesquite trees. Their hiding places might not have served them very well in broad daylight, but in the early morning gloom, they could stay hidden long enough to pour a deadly rain of rifle fire into the soldiers who got off the train. One of the outlaws had even climbed on top of the water tank and flattened himself on its wooden lid, so that he could take care of the brakeman whose job it would be to swing the long spout over from the tank to the locomotive.

Longarm had to suppress a groan. He had to give Vickery credit: The colonel had come up with a workable, if murderous, plan. In a matter of minutes, as soon as the train came to a stop and the Vice President and his escort disembarked, bloody hell would break loose.

Vickery had put on his hat and coat, tipping the headgear at a rakish angle. He was grinning broadly as he stood beside Longarm. Niland was right behind the marshal, the barrel of his gun jabbed uncomfortably in Longarm's back.

"You see, Marshal, my plan is going to work after all," Vickery boasted. "I knew all along you couldn't stop this mission from succeeding. That's why I was willing to let you live to see this. It's a momentous occasion, you know. You might even say historic."

Longarm didn't say anything. He wasn't going to give Vickery the satisfaction.

The train was well within sight by now, rolling inexorably along the tracks toward Inferno. Its whistle shrilled again, louder this time because it was closer. Longarm grimaced at the sound.

Vickery looked so proud he was fit to bust as the train pulled up to the station. The crew would figure that he and Vickery and Niland were some sort of welcoming committee, thought Longarm. They wouldn't realize what was going on until it was too late.

Unless he could manage to warn them somehow, even if it meant risking his own life . . .

Niland must have read his mind. The major dug the barrel of the pistol even harder against Longarm's spine and said, "This gun is cocked and ready, Long. You make any move and I'll lift my thumb off the hammer. It'll blow your backbone right in two."

And his own body would muffle the shot, Longarm realized, to the point that nobody on the train would be able to hear it over the hiss of steam, the squeal of brakes, and the clatter of fittings. He would be throwing his life away for nothing.

The big locomotive with its diamond stack came to a shuddering halt. The engine was even with the elevated tank so that it could take on water, while the first car had drawn to a stop next to the small platform in front of the station. Longarm and Niland stayed at the rear of the platform while Vickery strode forward, his back straight, ready to see his plan through to what he considered its glorious conclusion. Longarm bit back a curse of frustration as the blue-suited conductor climbed down rather awkwardly from the first car. The man's cap was pulled down low over his forehead, and he hadn't looked up yet to see Vickery striding toward him. Vickery was reaching for his gun.

Longarm opened his mouth to yell a warning, even though he knew full well it was going to cost him his life.

At the same instant, the conductor finally looked up, and somehow there was a gun in his hand as he lifted it, causing Vickery to stop in his tracks. The conductor pulled back the hammer of the little pistol and pointed the barrel right between Vickery's eyes, which were wide with shock.

"Don't move, Colonel," said Judge Hiram Schofield, "or I'll blow your goddamn brains out."

Longarm was just about as surprised as Vickery, but he had the presence of mind to feel the barrel of Niland's pistol move away from his back as the major tried to bring it to bear on Schofield. Twisting sharply, Longarm drove his elbow back into Niland's belly and knocked the gun aside in the same motion. The pistol cracked, and the bullet ricocheted off the side of one of the railroad cars.

"Open fire!" Vickery screamed.

Some of his men probably knew that something had gone wrong, while others doubtless did not. But all of them followed the colonel's order and started raking the train with rifle fire. A volley crashed from inside the train, however, and that return fire was deadly. The soldiers accompanying the Vice President had not been caught in the open, as Vickery had planned. They were behind sturdy cover in the coaches, and their bullets downed several of the outlaws.

Meanwhile, Longarm was struggling with Niland while Vickery lunged at Schofield. The judge jerked the trigger of the pistol in his hand, but Vickery had already ducked under the barrel. The bullet plucked Vickery's hat from his head, but that was all the damage it did. The next instant, Vickery crashed into Schofield, sending both of them staggering back against the rear platform of the car from which Schofield had just disembarked.

Longarm had hold of Niland's wrist with his left hand and was keeping the major from bringing the gun to bear again. With his other fist, he launched an uppercut that Niland was unable to deflect. The blow landed solidly, knocking Niland backward. Longarm twisted savagely on his

160

opponent's wrist, and Niland finally dropped the gun. It fell to the station platform, where Longarm's boot accidentally struck it and sent it skidding away out of reach.

Vickery had his hands wrapped around Schofield's throat and was banging the judge's head against the iron steps attached to the coach platform. A shout of "Vickery!" made him glance up in time to see Faye McCormick standing above him on the platform, a gun clutched in both of her hands to steady it. She pulled the trigger.

The pistol cracked wickedly. Vickery let go of Schofield and staggered back as the bullet dug a shallow but painful furrow across his side. He caught his balance, jerked his own gun from its holster, and fired at Faye, who yelped in alarm and ducked back into the railroad car.

Still gasping for breath from being choked so brutally, Schofield barreled into Vickery, tackling him around the waist. They fell to the platform and began rolling over and over.

Longarm still had his hands full with Niland. The two men were slugging it out, trading blow for blow, each of them absorbing about as much damage as he was dishing out. Longarm had an advantage in height and reach, but Niland was somewhat fresher and not as exhausted. Longarm's arms felt like lead as he threw punch after punch. He sensed that if he didn't finish this soon, he wouldn't like the way it ended.

In his battle with Schofield, Vickery's hand rose and fell, holding his revolver, and when the gun landed with a thud on the judge's head, Schofield shuddered and lay still. Vickery scrambled to his feet, looming over the unconscious judge.

Longarm threw a roundhouse right that staggered Niland. While the major was off balance, Longarm landed a left jab that pulped Niland's nose and sent blood spurting over Longarm's knuckles. Setting himself, Longarm hooked a right to Niland's belly, doubling the man over. A left cross with everything Longarm had behind it jerked Niland's head to the side and finished him off. Out cold, Niland fell, sprawling on the platform at Longarm's feet.

"Custis!" Faye screamed from the train.

Longarm's head snapped around. He saw Vickery about to pump a slug into Schofield and threw himself toward the gun Niland had dropped. It was a long dive, but he had time to make it because Faye's cry had distracted Vickery. Seeing Longarm going for the gun, Vickery swung away from Schofield with a snarl and triggered a shot at the marshal.

Longarm's hand slapped the butt of the gun as Vickery's bullet chewed splinters from the station platform next to his head. He tipped up the barrel of the weapon and pulled the trigger. Vickery staggered but didn't go down. The colonel fired again, then stumbled toward the cab of the engine.

Vickery's second shot had missed as well, and Longarm was tired but unhurt as he scrambled to his feet. He threw a glance along the length of the train to see how the battle was going between the soldiers and Vickery's men. Most of the outlaws appeared to be either dead or badly wounded already, and the soldiers were pouring off the train to start mopping up.

One of the troopers suddenly grabbed his chest and collapsed in a staggering fall as a shot blasted from somewhere above Longarm's head. Longarm looked up and saw the outlaw who had been posted on top of the water tank blazing away at the soldiers, taking advantage of the high position. Longarm lifted the gun in his hand and squeezed off a shot.

The outlaw dropped his rifle, clutched his midsection, and doubled over from the impact of the marshal's bullet. He pitched off the water tank and plummeted to the ground to lie in a bloody, shapeless heap beside the tracks.

Longarm looked toward the engine in time to see Vickery leaping into the cab. He didn't know what the colonel was up to, but he was damned if he was going to let Vickery get away after this unexpected turn of events. Longarm wanted to check on Schofield and find out if the judge was still alive, and he was anxious to see Faye again as well, to make certain she was all right. But finishing the fight with Vickery was going to have to come first. Longarm took a step toward the cab.

The train gave a lurch and shuddered into motion.

"Son of a bitch!" Longarm exclaimed as his eyes widened in surprise. Vickery was stealing the damned train!

And Longarm wondered suddenly if the Vice President was still on board.

He broke into a run, intending to leap onto the platform of the first car, but before he could reach it, Vickery leaned out from the cab and blasted a shot at him. Longarm felt a giant hand slap at his leg and knock him down. He spun to the platform and grabbed his left thigh. Blood seeped between his fingers, but he could tell the wound, painful as it might be, wasn't serious. Vickery's slug had simply burned a crease on his thigh.

But the shot had done its job. The train was picking up speed, and Longarm knew he wouldn't be able to get aboard now. He struggled to his feet and threw a couple of futile shots at the cab, but from this angle, all his bullets did was flatten themselves against the coal tender. Longarm cursed bitterly.

His voice took on a tone of desperation as he saw Faye staring at him from the platform of the first car. "Jump!" he yelled at her. "Jump, damn it!" The train was still going slow enough so that a leap from it wouldn't be risking much more than a few bumps and bruises, a broken leg at worst.

But Faye stayed where she was, clutching the iron railing around the platform and looking scared. Even after all she had gone through, she couldn't find the nerve to jump off of a moving train.

"Son of a bitch!" Longarm bit out. Still holding his wounded leg, he turned around and looked for somebody in charge of the soldiers, most of whom appeared to have been caught off the train when it began moving. He spotted a man wearing a captain's uniform and hobbled toward him.

Several of the troopers saw him coming and threw up their rifles, aiming at him. Longarm realized belatedly that, to them, he must look like another of the outlaws. He bent over hurriedly, placed the gun on the ground, and straightened with his hands in the air.

"Hold on!" he called urgently. "I'm United States Deputy Marshal Custis Long."

The captain stalked up to him, covering him with a pistol. "Do you have any proof of that, mister?"

"He . . . he's who he says he is, Captain," croaked a voice behind Longarm. He glanced over his shoulder to see Schofield sitting up, rubbing his bruised throat.

The officer lowered his gun. "Well, then, what can I do for you, Marshal? I have problems of my own, you know. That renegade's getting away with the train."

"And a lady," said Longarm. "Is the Vice President still on board?"

"No, sir. He's safe and sound several miles back up the line. I'm going to send a buggy out to fetch him as soon as we get everything squared away here."

"You left him out there alone?" asked Longarm.

Schofield limped up beside him. "No, some of those soldier blues are still with him," rasped the judge. "He'll be safe enough. Vickery's going the opposite direction, and all of his men are either dead or prisoners here."

"He's got Faye," Longarm said grimly, "and I need a horse."

"A horse?" Schofield said. "A horse can't outrun that train. Look, the damned thing's almost out of sight already. It's impossible!"

Longarm glanced along the tracks to the west and saw that Schofield was telling the truth. "Then I'm wasting time," he snapped. "One of you gents saddle me a horse, the fastest one you can find." He reached down and picked up the gun he had placed on the ground a few minutes earlier. "I've got a train to catch."

Impossible or not, he intended to do it.

Chapter 18

While a couple of the troopers hurried down to the livery stable to throw a saddle on a horse, Longarm said to Schofield, "Claude and some other fellas are locked up in the jail. I reckon I can count on you to let 'em out?"

"I'll take care of it," Schofield answered. "What are you going to do?"

"Are there any shortcuts along the route west of here, any place where the rails make a big curve?"

Schofield tugged at his ginger-colored beard in concentration. "I see what you're getting at," he said. "There's a place where the tracks swing to the south to bypass some mesas, then the route angles north again. That's rugged country in between, though. I'm not sure you could make good enough time to catch up to the train."

"I've got to try," said Longarm. "I'm not going to let Vickery get away now."

"And there's Mrs. McCormick to think of too," Schofield added. "Why don't I come with you?"

Longarm shook his head. "I can travel faster by myself, Judge. No offense."

"None taken, my boy." Schofield's face hardened. "Just get that bastard." He hesitated. "Long, I . . . I'm sorry about what happened yesterday afternoon. I know I'll probably have to face some charges over my part in this whole affair, but that's all right.''

''We'll see, Judge.'' The troopers were leading a horse toward the station, a long-legged black that looked to have both speed and sand. Longarm sure as hell hoped that was the case.

He scavenged a couple of extra six-guns and tucked them behind his belt, then swung up into the saddle of the black. The captain said, ''I can commandeer some more horses and send some of my men with you, Marshal.''

''Send 'em along behind,'' Longarm said. ''Right now, I can't wait.''

With that, he dug his heels into the flanks of the horse and sent it leaping forward into a gallop.

The train was completely out of sight by now, even though only a few minutes had passed since it pulled out of Inferno. Longarm's keen eyes searched the landscape in front of him as he raced along beside the railroad tracks, but he couldn't see any sign of his quarry. He hoped the horse was well rested. They might be in for a long run.

Several miles out of town, he suddenly spotted something up ahead, lying beside the tracks, and his heart thudded painfully in his chest when he realized it was a body. Had Faye finally leaped from the speeding train, only to be crushed and broken by the impact of her landing?

As he drew closer, however, he could tell that the body wasn't that of a woman. It was a man, and the overalls and cap told Longarm it was probably the engineer. Longarm galloped up to the man and reined the black to a halt, swinging down out of the saddle as he did so. He dropped to one knee beside the engineer, who was still alive.

''Glad to . . . see you . . . mister,'' the engineer grated through teeth clenched against the pain going through him. ''Figure I . . . busted my leg . . . when I landed.''

''What happened?'' asked Longarm. ''Did you jump out of the cab?''

''That . . . sumbitch . . . made me jump. Said he could . . . run the engine . . . didn't need me no more.'' The engineer caught hold of Longarm's sleeve. ''He tied the throttle down

. . . said he was going to . . . cut the cars loose . . ."

"Can he do that?"

The engineer nodded. "Sure . . . tracks run straight for . . . several more miles. He'd have time to . . . climb over the coal tender and . . . pull the couplin' pin . . . then get back in the cab 'fore . . . 'fore the route swings south."

Longarm nodded and told the man, "I'm afraid I've got to leave you here for now, old-timer. But there'll be some soldiers along in a few minutes, and they'll take care of you."

"You got to . . . stop that train . . ."

"I intend to," Longarm vowed. He started to stand up.

The engineer's fingers hooked even more tightly into the marshal's arm. "You don't . . . understand. We didn't . . . take on no water . . . back in Inferno. Boiler's goin' to over-heat . . . if that fella keeps on . . . pushin' it so hard. Liable to . . . blow the hell out of it."

Longarm's eyes widened. The engineer was right. And if the boiler on the locomotive blew up, the train would derail violently, probably killing everybody on board. That might be a fitting end for Thaddeus Vickery, but if Faye was still on the train with him . . .

"I'll stop him," Longarm promised the engineer as he got to his feet. "Count on that, old-timer."

He mounted up again, already regretting the few minutes he had spent here in conversation with the injured man. And yet, he knew more about the situation now than he had before. He knew just how desperate it really was. He pushed the black for more speed.

A few minutes later, he spied something on the tracks ahead. It came as no surprise to Longarm when he recognized the caboose and several cars of the train. Vickery had obviously made good on his plan to uncouple the engine and the coal tender from the cars. As Longarm swept closer, he saw several blue-uniformed figures standing alongside the stalled train. Some of the civilian passengers were outside walking around too.

Longarm galloped up and reined in again, walking the horse across to the north side of the tracks. One of the soldiers hailed him, and without dismounting, Longarm called, "Your captain and the rest of your bunch will be coming along directly. Anybody hurt bad here?"

A beefy man with sergeant's stripes on his sleeves shook his head. "A few bullet wounds," said the non-com, "but nothing serious. Who the hell are you, mister?"

"U.S. Deputy Marshal Long. I'm after the fella who stole that engine."

"He cut us loose before we could get up there to the cab," said the sergeant. "We figured from the way the train took off from Inferno that something was wrong."

"You were right about that," Longarm said. "The son of a bitch who planned that business back in town is the one who took the engine."

"And the first coach."

Longarm's jaw tensed. "What did you say?"

"He uncoupled the cars right behind the first passenger coach," explained the sergeant. "What's wrong, Marshal?"

"Do you have a woman with you?"

"Pretty young woman in a red dress, the one who was with that judge from Inferno when they stopped us?" The sergeant shook his head. "I haven't seen her, Marshal."

Longarm didn't waste any more time talking. He kicked the black into a run again with a shout and ignored the questions yelled after him by the startled non-com.

Faye had been in that first coach, and evidently she still was. Vickery still had her, probably thinking he would use her as a hostage if he had to.

And even though neither one of them likely knew it, they were riding on a massive bomb that was just waiting to go off. . . .

He had forced her at gunpoint to climb over the coal that was piled in the tender, and her red dress was ruined forever—which she might not care about much longer, Faye reflected bitterly. Her hands and legs were stained from the coal, and there were streaks and smudges of ebony across her face where she had brushed her hair back with her fingers. Vickery was in much the same condition.

"We look like we ought to be in a minstrel show," he said with a grin as he stood at the controls of the locomotive, one hand on the throttle and the other hand filled with the gun he was using to cover her.

Faye didn't say anything. She didn't want to talk to him, didn't want to even acknowledge his existence.

When the train had lurched into motion and pulled out of the station, rapidly picking up speed, she wasn't sure at first what was going on. But then she had seen Longarm on the platform of the station, had seen him fall to a shot fired from the cab of the locomotive, and had figured it out. Vickery was stealing the train and making his getaway in it.

She had tried to force herself to leap from the coach, she really had. But fear had rooted her feet to the platform until it was much too late to do anything. Then, when her stunned brain had finally realized that she could go back into the other cars with the soldiers who were still on the train, it was too late again.

Vickery had appeared in the front door of the passenger car, gun in hand, his face twisted by an evil leer. She was the only one in the coach, and he had covered her with the Colt while he walked the length of the coach to the rear, leaned down between the swaying cars, and pulled the coupling pin. The rest of the train had immediately started falling behind, slowed down by its great weight.

Faye had thought about leaping on him then and trying to knock him off the car, but the menacing barrel of Vickery's gun held her back. Then he had told her they were going up to the cab, and the nightmare in which she seemed to be caught had gotten even worse. She would never forget the terror that had coursed through her as she climbed over the coal tender toward the cab with an armed madman right behind her.

Once they were in the cab, Vickery had untied the throttle and taken over control of the engine again, slowing its speed as they approached a big bend to the south. Faye saw half a dozen rugged mesas jutting up from the land in front of them, the terrain forcing the alteration of the railroad's route.

Vickery handled the controls well, and the train took the curve smoothly.

"You can't get away, you know," Faye said as she stood as far away from him in the cab as she could. "The people back in Inferno will just wire the next stop. There'll be plenty of lawmen there to arrest you when we get there."

"I doubt that," Vickery said confidently. "When they see that you're with me, they'll back off. I'll demand horses for us, and we'll be across the border before anybody can stop us." His face hardened. "This mission may have been sabotaged, but there'll be another day for Colonel Thaddeus Vickery. You can count on that, my dear."

Faye tried not to shudder with revulsion. The worst part about it was that Vickery was probably right. By using her as a hostage and shield, he stood at least a chance of getting away.

She wondered how badly Longarm was hurt. A part of her wanted to believe that he would come after her, that he would save her from this lunatic. But she knew how unlikely that was. Inferno was a long way behind them now. The sun was up, and the cab was starting to get a little warm.

"I'm curious," said Vickery, breaking into her reverie. "I thought when the train showed up in Inferno that you and Schofield hadn't been able to stop it. What happened?"

Faye swallowed. She might as well talk to him, she decided. She didn't want him going crazy on her. "The train almost didn't stop," she said, raising her voice so that she could be heard over the rumble and clatter of the engine. "In fact, it went right past us before it finally stopped. The army had an officer in the cab with the engineer, and he was afraid we were trying to trick them into some sort of trap. But the engineer recognized Judge Schofield at the last minute and talked the officer into letting him stop to see what was going on. They figured something must be wrong up ahead in Inferno . . . and they were right, weren't they?"

"So Schofield tricked me by disguising himself as the conductor. *He* set a trap for *me*." Vickery shook his head in admiration. "Very smart, I have to admit it. What happened to the Vice President?"

"We left him several miles out of town with some of the troops. He's probably been brought into Inferno by now. The Mexican representative may even be there."

"I wouldn't doubt it," said Vickery. He sighed. "Ah, well, I still say it was a good plan. It could have worked." He shot a hard glance at her. "Without so much damned interference."

Faye tossed her hair back defiantly. "We couldn't just let you get away with it."

"Why didn't you stay with the Vice President?"

She didn't lie to him. "I wanted to see you captured."

Vickery laughed humorlessly. "Well, then, you were disappointed, weren't you?"

She didn't answer him. There was nothing left to say.

With her arms folded across her chest, she stared out at the mostly barren landscape rolling past. They had skirted the mesas to the south, and now the tracks were angling north again.

Movement caught her eye. She turned her gaze toward the rugged country to the right of the tracks and saw a small black dot moving against the brown and tan background. It almost looked like . . . it *was* a figure on horseback.

A rider, galloping toward the rail line on a course that was obviously meant to intercept the tracks.

Faye's breath caught in her throat. She knew how unlikely it was, but she couldn't deny the hope welling up inside her. If that distant figure was Longarm . . .

Vickery might be in for one more surprise.

Longarm leaned forward in the saddle, calling out soft-voiced encouragement to the magnificent horse underneath him. The black had proved to be as game a mount as Longarm had ever ridden. It had given him all it had during the dash through the mesa country, blending speed with sure-footedness. The soldiers who had picked out the horse at the livery barn had shown good judgment. Longarm wondered who the black belonged to—and if the gent would consider selling the animal.

171

When he passed the last of the craggy, upthrust tablelands and started back out onto the flats, Longarm's eyes searched desperately for any sign of the train. His heart leaped as he saw the smoke rising from the stack and the train itself rolling along the tracks ahead of him. He tried to figure distances and angles, and he knew it would be tight.

But he stood a chance of intercepting the train. He was sure of that.

And a chance was all he needed.

"If you've got anything left, I need it now, old son!" he called to the horse. "Let's catch that train!"

As if understanding his words, the black lunged ahead, drawing even more speed from its exhausted body. Longarm hoped the horse's heart didn't burst from the strain. After the race it had run, it deserved better than that—and he deserved a chance to finally settle the score with Vickery.

"What the hell?" Vickery exploded as he looked off to the right.

He had spotted Longarm, Faye thought. That was what she had been afraid of. The rider was close enough now that she could recognize the rangy federal lawman, and the hope she'd felt had grown until it filled her.

Now Vickery extended his gun hand out the window of the cab and started firing. He emptied his pistol at the approaching rider, then cursed when the shots seemed to have no effect. Longarm was still out of range.

Vickery jammed his gun back in its holster and quickly retied a length of cord around the throttle to hold it down. Faye watched him, wide-eyed, then saw him reach for his gun again. He was probably planning to reload, and eventually Longarm would be close enough to be in danger from those shots.

Without waiting any longer, Faye threw herself at Vickery's back.

She hoped she might be able to knock him out of the cab, but as she crashed into him he caught his balance and set his feet. She reached around his head and tried to claw his eyes with her fingernails, but with a roar of rage, he swung his arm around and backhanded her. The vicious blow cracked across her face and sent her sailing backward to smash into the front wall of the coal tender. She slumped and almost fell, catching herself with one hand against the door where coal could be shoveled out of the tender.

"I'll kill you if you try that again!" Vickery screamed at her. Obviously, he had forgotten about his plan to use her as a hostage when they reached the next settlement. He had more urgent problems now, in the person of Deputy Marshal Custis Long.

Faye's cheek throbbed where he had struck her. She watched as he shook the spent cartridges from his revolver and thumbed fresh shells into the cylinder. He snapped it closed and grinned bleakly at her. "Your Marshal Long is going to get a warm welcome," he promised as he swung back toward the side of the cab and the window beside the controls.

The next instant, a curse ripped from him. Faye was just as startled as she looked out of the cab.

Longarm was gone.

So damned close, Longarm thought wildly, but not quite close enough.

The train had roared past before he could reach the rails. All he could do was swing in behind it and hope the horse still had enough strength and speed left in its body. He galloped alongside the tracks, calling to the animal, pleading with it to give its utmost.

The black responded one final time, its legs flashing as it ran all out, covering seemingly incredible lengths of ground with each stride. Slowly, maddeningly slowly, the gap between horse and train grew smaller. Longarm leaned to the side, reaching for the railing around the rear platform of the passenger car.

"A little more, old son!" he cried. "Just a little more!"

There would be only one chance to do this right. Longarm waited and waited as seconds dragged by and the gap shrank a little more. Then the railing was within reach, and he kicked his feet free of the stirrups and leaped.

His hand closed around the iron rail and clamped shut with a grip like a vise. He got his other hand on the railing and hung there, his legs drawn up so they wouldn't drag on the roadbed. Pain shot through his arms and shoulders and his lips drew back from his teeth in a grimace of effort as he struggled to pull himself up.

Then his booted feet found purchase on the framework of the car, and he was able to haul himself up and over the railing. He sprawled on the platform, his muscles screaming and quivering, and drew in great gulping breaths of air.

Longarm wasn't sure how long he lay there. It couldn't have been very long before the urgency of the situation prodded him to his feet. He had to stop the train before the engine exploded.

Drawing one of the guns he had brought along, he staggered over to the door of the coach, opened it, and hurried along its length to the front door. There was a platform there too, and it was as empty as the rest of the coach. Beyond the platform was the rear of the coal tender. The steel rungs of a ladder beckoned him.

Longarm put the gun away again, grasped the ladder, and started climbing. His pulse was hammering wildly in his head. Cinders from the smokestack stung his eyes. Lack of sleep had already made his eyeballs feel like they had been plucked from their sockets, rolled around in sand for a while, then stuck back in his head. If he was alive when this was all over, he vowed himself, he was going to sleep for a week.

He made it to the top of the ladder and scrambled over into the heap of coal that filled the tender. When he lifted his head, he could see Vickery standing at the controls of the engine. The renegade colonel had his head turned away from Longarm; he was watching the tracks in front of the train.

Longarm had seen Vickery shooting at him earlier. The colonel must have decided that Longarm had fallen behind the train and been unable to catch up. He would soon find out just how wrong he was. But where was Faye? Longarm asked himself. He couldn't see her, and anxiety gnawed at him. He started scrambling over the coal on hands and knees.

As he drew closer to the front of the tender, he saw that the throttle was still tied down. Vickery was paying no attention to the gauges in front of him. Obviously, he didn't know as much about railroading as he thought he did. Even from where Longarm crouched atop the heap of coal, he could see that the needles of several of the gauges were already in the red danger area.

And speaking of red, he thought crazily, Faye had been wearing a red dress when he saw her last. There it was again as Vickery reached back and hauled her forward in the cab, the dress's original color still visible in places underneath black smears from the coal. Vickery turned his head and said something to her, although Longarm couldn't hear the words over the noise of the engine. Vickery was smirking and laughing, and Longarm was willing to bet he was gloating again.

Longarm drew one of the guns and moved forward, about to give Vickery the surprise of his life.

The coal suddenly rolled and shifted under Longarm's feet. He sat down hard, and the noise the chunks of coal caused as they tumbled and slid made Vickery's head snap around. The colonel's eyes widened in shock as he saw Longarm. Vickery's left arm shot out and looped around Faye's neck as his right hand flashed to the gun on his hip. He jerked Faye against him as a shield.

"Long!" he screamed. "Damn you! Why won't you die and leave me alone!"

Longarm couldn't fire for fear of hitting Faye. But Vickery didn't have to worry about such things. His gun came up and belched flame as Longarm threw himself to the side, trying to get out of the way of the shot.

The bullet drew a line of pain along his forearm like a finger made of fire before thudding into the pile of coal. Longarm's muscles spasmed, and the gun slipped from his fingers.

"Noooo!" Faye shrieked. She twisted around in Vickery's grip, desperation giving her strength, and this time her

175

fingernails found his eyes. Vickery cried out and flung his arm up to ward her off, giving Faye the chance to tear herself away from him.

Longarm's arm hurt like the dickens, but as Faye threw herself to one side, out of the line of fire, the marshal dove off the tender and crashed into Vickery. Both of them fell back against the controls of the train. Longarm grabbed Vickery's wrist and slammed his gun hand against the door of the firebox. The colonel screamed wildly and dropped the pistol as the hot door seared his flesh.

Longarm drove his elbow up underneath Vickery's chin and jolted his head back. Without looking around, Longarm shouted, "Faye! Get out of here! Go back over the coal!"

He wasn't sure if she would do as he said or not, and he couldn't check because he had his hands full with Vickery. Fighting like the madman he was, Vickery threw wild punches and panted and snarled curses. Longarm warded off as many of the blows as he could, and finally straightened Vickery up with a swift combination of punches. Vickery hung there against the controls, half-stunned.

That gave Longarm a chance to fling a glance over his shoulder and see that Faye was scrambling toward safety over the coal. There was no real safety on this train, however, as long as the engine was overheated almost to the point of bursting. Longarm looked at the gauges he could see. All of the needles were pegged out.

The catastrophe was beyond stopping, Longarm thought. The engine was going to blow at any second. His only chance, and it was a slim one, would be to uncouple the tender from the engine and let the doomsday locomotive go on its way down the tracks. He spun toward the coupling.

With an incoherent cry, Vickery landed on his back. The colonel was completely insane now, his mind unhinged by everything that had happened. He and Longarm sprawled on the floor of the cab. Vickery got his arm around Longarm's neck, and it was like an iron bar on Longarm's throat, cutting off his air.

A red haze swam before Longarm's eyes. He and Vickery were lying at the rear of the cab, and the coupling was still within Longarm's reach. Fighting not to black out, he slipped his arm down into the narrow gap between the engine and the tender. If the train jolted right now, the gap might pinch together and take his arm off at the shoulder, but it was a risk he had to take. His fingers searched for the coupling pin.

In the meantime, Vickery was doing his damnedest to choke Longarm to death. That red mist was getting thicker and thicker, clogging his vision. But there wasn't much to see in this position anyway, Longarm thought crazily, only the riveted steel plates of the cab's floor.

His fingertips touched the ring at the top of the coupling pin.

Somehow, he found the strength to grasp the pin and pull. It resisted at first, then popped free suddenly.

"Die!" screamed Vickery. "Die, damn you!"

Longarm drove his other elbow up and back, into Vickery's midsection. He put all the strength he had left into the blow, and it weakened Vickery's grip enough so that Longarm could arch his back and buck the colonel off.

The gap between the tender and the engine was already a couple of feet. Longarm struggled up onto his hands and knees and tried to get his feet underneath him. From the top of the coal, Faye had seen what was going on, and she cried, "Jump, Custis, jump!" Longarm came up into a crouch and flung himself toward the tender, reaching out for the rungs of the ladder on this end.

He caught them and then slammed against the tender, but he managed to hang on with both hands. His feet found one of the lower rungs, and he hung there shaking, utterly drained. The tender and the passenger car behind it were slowing down dramatically as the engine pulled away from them.

"Custis, look out!" screamed Faye. "Vickery!"

Longarm turned his head and saw that the colonel had gotten back up onto his knees inside the cab. Not only that, but he had regained the gun he had dropped earlier. He lifted the weapon now, a savage, insane grin on his coal-smudged features, and eared back the hammer as he pointed the gun at Longarm. Vickery was laughing as he started to squeeze the trigger, and the only thing Longarm could do was hang there on the front end of the tender and watch in horror.

Behind Vickery, the cab seemed to open up like the petals of a flower blooming in hell. Fire erupted from the exploding engine and engulfed the colonel. He vanished in an instant as the explosion ripped the engine into a million pieces.

Longarm turned his head as debris slammed into the tender. Vickery was gone, utterly consumed in the blast, but Longarm and Faye weren't safe yet. The tender and the passenger car could still derail. Longarm squeezed his eyes shut and hoped the Good Lord still had a soft spot in his heart for old boys from West-by-God Virginia.

The tender shuddered to a stop about ten feet from the spot where the rails had been twisted and destroyed by the explosion.

Longarm opened his eyes, aware that somebody was calling his name rather frantically. He blinked something out of his eyes, and realized it was blood from a cut on his forehead. In fact, he was bleeding all over from cuts and gashes caused by the debris flung out by the exploding locomotive. But he was alive, and he was grinning as he looked up into Faye's blackened, worried face. She was extending a hand to him, saying, "Custis! Are you all right? Custis . . . !"

Longarm reached up and took her hand, feeling her soft fingers fold around his. . . .

Chapter 19

Longarm held on tightly as she stepped delicately over the side of the big tin tub, into the hot, soapy water.

"I already had a bath," said Faye with a giggle, "but I don't suppose another one will hurt me."

From Longarm's vantage point as he sat up in the tub, the triangle of fine-spun, curly chestnut hair between her thighs was right in front of his face. He leaned toward it, inhaling the clean, womanly scent of her.

Faye put her hands on his shoulders to steady herself as he nuzzled against her. "Oh, my," she said. "Custis, what are you—oh, my!"

She spread her thighs to let his lips and tongue roam among the folds of female flesh. After a moment, she warned him breathlessly, "I'm going to . . . slip and fall if you keep on . . . keep on doing that!"

"Wouldn't want you to hurt yourself," Longarm said with a grin. "Not after all we've been through. Sit down here with me."

He helped her sit down straddling his legs. She reached under the suds in the water between them and found his shaft, which was fully erect. Fisting one hand around it, she began pumping leisurely.

"Not too much of that now," Longarm cautioned.

"You certainly recovered your vitality in a hurry," she said. "This morning you claimed you were going to sleep until next month."

"A week, that's what I said."

"It's only been about ten hours."

He shrugged his broad shoulders. "I guess it's all that clean living I do."

Faye giggled again, leaned forward and kissed him, and continued to caress his stalk underneath the water.

As a matter of fact, Longarm *had* regained his strength a lot faster than he had expected to. Once he and Faye had gotten back to Inferno with the soldiers, he'd had the local sawbones patch up the bullet creases on his leg and arm and sew up the gash on his forehead. While that was going on, Longarm had discovered that the black horse which had run such a gallant race in pursuit of the train belonged to Schofield, which came as no surprise. With the iron grip he'd had on the town, it stood to reason that the best horse in these parts belonged to him too. Under the circumstances, the judge had said that he might just make a gift of the animal to Longarm, and Longarm had warned him not to consider it a bribe.

"Why, such a thought never entered my mind," Schofield had insisted, sounding somewhat offended.

Longarm and Faye had caught up on everything during the ride back to Inferno, so he knew how Schofield had come to be dressed as the conductor when the train rolled into the station. The surviving outlaws, including Niland, were locked up in the jail, and Vice President Wheeler was safely ensconced elsewhere in the hotel with plenty of guards around him while he had his meeting with that diplomat from Mexico City. Before that, however, the Vice President had taken a few moments to thank Longarm, Faye, and Schofield personally.

"You're mighty welcome," Longarm had told the politician. "And I may be calling on you for a kind word on my behalf when my boss in Denver, Chief Marshal Billy Vail, finds out I'm not bringing back the prisoner he sent me down here to fetch."

"I'll post a letter to Marshal Vail as soon as I'm back in Washington," Wheeler promised. "I think he'll be forgiving when he finds out how you saved both myself and the Mexican representative from great danger."

"Well, we can only hope," Longarm replied rather dubiously.

Schofield had spoken up then, asking the Vice President what Rutherford B. Hayes's policy was regarding executive clemency for crimes committed on a local level, and Longarm had left them there to hash that out.

Then he had cleaned up a little, crawled between some clean sheets in a hotel room, and immediately fallen into a deep sleep that had lasted until a little while earlier this evening. He had awaken ravenously hungry, and there was only one thing he could do to satisfy that hunger.

He'd gone to Claude's, of course.

Faye had been there, just as he'd hoped, and they had eaten together, then come back to the hotel, and now they were sitting together in a tub of hot water, which was just about the most pleasant circumstance Longarm could have contemplated.

"Do you realize it's only been thirty-six hours since you first rode into Inferno?" Faye asked. "Only a day and a half."

"A *busy* day and a half," Longarm corrected.

"Very busy. And we're about to make love for the third time in that day and a half."

"Are we?"

She lifted herself a little, moved closer to him, and settled down on his shaft, letting it fill her. "We are," she said throatily.

Longarm cupped her breasts, slick with soapsuds, as her hips began to pump up and down. Her pelvis ground against his. Faye closed her eyes as she rode him, obviously relishing the sensation. Longarm brought his mouth to her left nipple and sucked the pebbled brown bud between his lips.

The door of the hotel room crashed open and Longarm looked up past Faye's suds-dappled shoulder to see Niland standing there, gun in hand. The outlaw's face was contorted with hate as he jerked the pistol up.

Longarm's hand was a blur as it darted to the chair next to the tub and scooped up the revolver he had left there. His other hand came down on the top of Faye's head and pushed her underneath the water, out of the way. Longarm couldn't beat Niland's shot, but the bullet missed him, humming past his ear. Then the gun in Longarm's hand bucked against his palm as it roared, and the slug drilled into Niland's chest, throwing him back out of the doorway to crash against the opposite wall of the hotel corridor. The gun slipped from his fingers and thudded to the carpet runner on the floor as Niland slowly slid down the wall, leaving a bloody smear on the flowered paper. His eyes were already glassy in death.

Faye came up out of the water, sputtering and gasping for breath.

Heavy footsteps pounded down the hall, and Longarm was ready to fire again if need be. But a familiar face appeared in the doorway as Judge Hiram Schofield peered around the jamb, holding a shotgun. "Sorry," Schofield grunted. "Didn't mean to disturb anything, folks. Anybody hurt in there?"

"We're fine," Longarm replied curtly. "What the hell is Niland doing here?"

Schofield discreetly averted his eyes as Faye tried to bury her nudity in the suds that were left in the tub. "What I'd like to know," declared the judge, "is what you did to my jail, Long. Nobody ever broke out of there until you came to Inferno, and now we can't seem to keep anybody locked up in there. I'm not sure how Niland here managed to get out, but at least we won't have to worry about it happening again. Reckon he'll be going to the undertaker's this time."

"Just get him out of here and shut the door," said Longarm, "and I'll be much obliged, Your Honor."

Schofield issued the orders to the men who had come with him, then swung the door shut with a chuckle, blocking off the view of the grisly task going on outside in the hall. Longarm put the revolver back on the chair, glad that it was a habit of his to have a gun within easy reach most of the time.

"Now," he said to Faye, "where were we?"

Her hair was wet from the dunking and hung loosely around her face. Longarm thought she was lovely. She sighed and said, "Custis, surely after that you don't expect me to—"

"It's all over," Longarm promised. "This time, it really is."

"You swear?"

"I swear," he said solemnly.

A smile tugged at her mouth. "Well, I suppose if you're sure . . ." She reached underneath the water again, brought his organ to her slippery entrance, and slid down on the thick pole of flesh. Her arms went around his neck, and she clutched him tightly, all over. Her breath came hot and fast against his neck.

Three times in thirty-six hours, thought Longarm as he embraced her. Not bad. He had done better, of course. Maybe he could send a wire to Billy Vail and convince his boss to let him stay on here for a day or two of "rest," just so he and Faye could find out what they were really capable of.

Seemed like Inferno wasn't such a bad place after all.